TOGE

Ellen and Dermid Craig had been separated for longer than they had been married—but circumstances had brought Ellen back from Canada to Scotland with their small son, to confront Dermid again. Was this Ellen's chance to rebuild their marriage, or was it too late? Did she want him back? And for that matter—*did Dermid want her*?

Books you will enjoy
by FLORA KIDD

PASSIONATE ENCOUNTER

Being more English than Spanish in her outlook, Caroline couldn't face being married to a man she didn't love. She ran off to the wilds of the Pyrenees to take refuge with her old nurse—but instead met a passionate stranger who was going to change her whole life, for better or worse...

CANADIAN AFFAIR

There were two 'extras' to Jessica's business trip to Canada—the chance of a holiday in that fascinating country, and the possibility of her pleasant friendship with her boss developing into something warmer. Until she met Simon Benson, a man she knew she could easily love. But she also knew nothing but hurt could come from loving Simon Benson...

MARRIAGE IN MEXICO

Sebastian Suarez had rescued Dawn from drowning off the coast of Mexico and then done her a further favour—which was why she had accepted his proposal of marriage. But it didn't take her long to fall in love with him—nor to realise that he had married her only as a smokescreen to conceal his affair with another woman...

CASTLE OF TEMPTATION

Ardgour on the West Coast of Scotland seemed just the place to Aline to sort herself out and make up her mind about George Lawson, who wanted to marry her—until she found out that Dominic Lietch was there too. For Dominic's presence could only complicate matters—and she sensed that he still had the power to hurt her as he had all those years ago...

TOGETHER AGAIN

BY

FLORA KIDD

MILLS & BOON LIMITED
17-19 FOLEY STREET
LONDON W1A 1DR

All the characters in this book have no existence outside the imagination of the Author, and have no relation whatsoever to anyone bearing the same name or names. They are not even distantly inspired by any individual known or unknown to the Author, and all the incidents are pure invention.

The text of this publication or any part thereof may not be reproduced or transmitted in any form or by any means, electronic or mechanical, including photocopying, recording, storage in an information retrieval system, or otherwise, without the written permission of the publisher.

This book is sold subject to the condition that it shall not, by way of trade or otherwise, be lent, resold, hired out or otherwise circulated without the prior consent of the publisher in any form of binding or cover other than that in which it is published and without a similar condition including this condition being imposed on the subsequent purchaser.

First published 1979
Australian copyright 1979
Philippine copyright 1979
This edition 1979

© Flora Kidd 1979

ISBN 0 263 73096 4

Set in Linotype Plantin 11 on 11½ pt.

Made and printed in Great Britain by
Richard Clay (The Chaucer Press), Ltd., Bungay, Suffolk

CHAPTER ONE

ONCE again the jet-liner climbed away from the land to circle over the sea. Dark grey clouds rolled past the oval windows of the aircraft, spattering the panes with raindrops. Peering down through a cloud which was rapidly disintegrating, Ellen Craig saw for the third time the white-whipped greyish-green waves of the sea flinging themselves at a sandy shore, then the smooth green of a golf course across which bronze and yellow leaves were scurrying before the wind slid by under the wing. Pine trees, perpetually bent over in one direction, swayed about a many-gabled, slate-roofed golf club house and small cars crawled along a narrow roadway wet with rain. From the control tower of the airport's terminal building a light flashed blindingly and regularly, then it too slid by as the aircraft banked and, turning once more nose to wind, made its approach to the runway.

It was the captain's third attempt at landing. As he had already explained, the westerly wind which had pushed the plane across the Atlantic Ocean from Canada so that it had reached the shores of Scotland ahead of schedule was now making landing difficult and if he couldn't land it safely this time he would fly on to Heathrow. Passengers who would normally have disembarked at Prestwick would be ferried back to Glasgow airport by British Airways' shuttle service.

Ellen didn't want that to happen. She was travelling with her nearly four-year-old son Rowan and, although he had slept nearly all night, he was now wide awake and very restless, obviously fed up with being confined in his seat. As for herself, she felt jaded after not having slept a wink during the flight, and her feet were swollen because she had foolishly taken off her new shoes and was now having difficulty slipping them on. She felt she wasn't in a fit state to cope with any change in arrangements.

So it was with a profound sense of relief that she saw the grey wet tarmac of the runway rushing up to meet the plane and the flat fields which surrounded the airport blurring before her eyes. She didn't even mind the jolt with which the wheels hit the runway, although Rowan objected noisily and asked if the plane had crashed.

After the quiet spaciousness of Mirabel airport, from which she had taken off the previous night, Prestwick airport seemed very small and chilly. To arrive after an all-night flight was not the best time to return to a country, thought Ellen, bleakly looking round at the other passengers who were walking with her towards the signs which indicated where passengers should go. Everyone looked like she felt, hollow-eyed, cold and rumpled.

It had been a mistake to travel in the black velvet suit. She had bought it because her mother had suggested she should wear something black to show she acknowledged the death of Neil Craig of Inchcullin even if she hadn't been able to attend his funeral. At Mirabel airport the suit had looked elegant; now it was crushed and was covered with tiny bits of fluff off the blanket which the steward had given her to cover Rowan with. And her silky oyster-coloured blouse had wilted. Instead of feeling and looking like a poised and coolly-collected television interviewer she felt and looked like the mother of a lively demanding four-year-old, worn out and close to defeat.

Pushing the three cases she had brought with her on a trolley, she searched the faces of the people who had come to meet disembarking passengers. There didn't seem to be anyone she recognised. No sign of the gaunt narrow face of James Blair, Neil Craig's chauffeur, whom she had expected to meet her. It looked as if she would have to find her own way to Inchcullin House. But how?

Standing in the main hallway of the airport building, she chewed at her lower lip, trying to remember the best way of travelling to Portcullin which was the nearest town to Inchcullin, on the coast of Kintyre. She knew she could drive round there. It was a long way, but she supposed she could make it if only she could hire a car. And having a car at her disposal would be an advantage, make her independent and able to please herself.

Looking around, she saw a sign pointing the way to the area of the airport where the car-rental people had their desks. There was a line-up at all three agencies. Ellen joined the shortest line, much to Rowan's annoyance, and he began to complain, pulling at her hand and whining that he wanted to go to the bathroom, clutching at his groin with a chubby hand and managing to look as if he were in great agony, although she was sure he couldn't be because he had gone to the toilet on the plane just before the aircraft had made its first approach to the airport.

Eventually she couldn't stand his whining any longer. She gave him a rough shake and told him to be quiet in her coldest, severest voice. Immediately he burst into tears and everyone who was waiting turned to look first at him, with sympathy, and then at her with censure, so that she seethed inwardly. If only some of them knew what it was like to be a single parent, to have to be both mother and father and hold a job down at the same time, it would be to her they would be showing the sympathy.

'Rowan, please be quiet!' she whispered pleadingly, squatting down before him.

'I wanna go home,' he wailed. 'I wanna go to Nanny's house!'

'But we can't go to Nanny's house right now,' she explained. 'We're in Scotland now, not in Ottawa, and you won't be able to go to Nanny's house until next Saturday when we get back there.'

'Wanna go now,' insisted Rowan.

'We can't. We have to go and see another lady first.'

'Another nanny?' he asked hopefully, opening wide his black-lashed, tear-washed dark brown gold-flecked eyes.

'No, not a nanny, an aunty.'

'Will she have candy?' he lisped. He couldn't say the letter 's' properly. It always came out sounding like 'th'.

'I expect she will.'

'Where does she live?'

'In a big house by the sea. The house is like a castle.'

'A real castle?' His eyes were now round with awe and his desire to go to Nanny's house was forgotten as was his desire to go to the bathroom. 'Is there a dragon in it?'

While she had been talking to him the people in front of her in the line-up had been provided with cars and the fair-haired young woman was waiting for her.

'And how long will you be needing the car?' asked the young woman in her soft sing-song Scottish voice after she had filled out the application form and had examined Ellen's driving licence.

'A week.'

'Returning it here?'

'Yes.'

'Ellen, what do you think you're doing?'

The voice which spoke beside her was familiar and had once been much loved. The sound of it caused her heart to leap and beat faster. Slowly she turned her head to look. He was there, leaning on the counter beside her, a tall man in a well-tailored suit of fine greenish tweed, and he was watching her with dark brown eyes which were deep-set under level black eyebrows. Her husband, Dermid Craig.

'I'm hiring a car,' she replied coolly. 'What are you doing here?'

'Meeting you,' he said surprisingly with an ironic quirk of his mouth.

'But I didn't see you waiting with the other people when I came off the plane.'

'I wasn't. I've only just arrived.'

'Mrs Craig, would you please sign this form and give me the name and address of someone living in this country who would act as a reference on your behalf,' said the young woman behind the counter.

'She won't be needing the car.' Dermid spoke with a cool authority which brooked no argument. 'Come on, Ellen, where's your luggage? I've got a car waiting outside to take us to Wemyss Bay.' His hand was under her elbow, urging her away from the desk, and she was aware of the young woman sighing and tearing up the form she had filled out.

'Aren't we going to the castle?' wailed Rowan, and promptly burst into tears again, bewildered by the strange new world in which he found himself and which seemed to have no relation to the world in which he normally lived, and for the first time Dermid Craig noticed his son. His eyes narrow between their lashes, his wide mouth compressed at one corner, he stared down at hair the tawny-gold colour of a rowan leaf in autumn and at tear-filled eyes the same colour as his own.

'Myself when young,' he murmured softly. Then his glance slanted in Ellen's direction. 'A castle?' he drawled with a satirical lift of one eyebrow.

'I told him the house is like a castle,' she replied defensively. 'Well, it is a bit like one with all those turrets, and it was the only way I could get him to stop crying.'

'Been playing you up, has he?' Little golden flecks of devilment began to flicker in his eyes as their glance roved slowly over her. 'You look as if you've been in a fight,' he remarked derisively. 'Who were you wrestling with all night? Him? Or your conscience?'

'Neither,' she retorted, one hand going to her hair to push it back from her forehead, then to the bow of her blouse to straighten it. Her fingers flicked futilely at the blanket fluff on the lapels of her suit jacket. Oh, why did he have to turn up when she was looking her worst? 'Dermid,' she said determinedly, 'I'm not going with you to Inchcullin.'

'No?' The black eyebrows which contrasted so unusually with his thick russet hair lifted in ironical surprise. 'Why not?'

'I'd rather travel by myself. I'll drive there.'

'It's a long way and would take you most of today. You wouldn't get there until after dark.' His glance went again to the sniffling child. 'A bit hard on him, too, but then I should have guessed you'd put yourself first.'

'I'm not putting myself first!' she exploded.

'I think you are,' he retorted, and squatted down in front of Rowan, placing his hands on the child's slight shoulders.

'Listen, laddie,' he said crisply, 'I've had quite

enough of your bawling and so has everyone else around here. You've made your point. Now, *shut up*!'

Much to Ellen's irritation Rowan obeyed immediately, stopped howling as abruptly as he had started, and there were no tears at all in the eyes which considered Dermid with interest. It looked very much as if the little devil had been playing her up.

'Who are you?' Rowan demanded.

'I'm your father. That mean anything to you?' replied Dermid.

'Yes,' Rowan lisped, and nodded his head. 'My friend Tony has a father. So has Barbara Ann,' he added, and putting his right thumb in his mouth he sucked it while he continued to stare at Dermid.

Dermid stayed in a squatting position for a few seconds staring back, then he slowly straightened up and looked at Ellen. There was an accusing expression in his eyes.

'He has a lisp and he sucks his thumb,' he said. 'What in God's name have you been doing to him, Ellen?'

'I haven't been doing anything to him,' she replied hotly, and looked around her. Nearly everyone had gone from the area near the car rental agency desks. The place looked deserted and bleak and she felt a damp coldness seeping into her.

She wished she had never come. She wished she had ignored the lawyer's letter which had requested she be present at a reading of the last will and testament of Neil Craig at Inchcullin House on October the thirty-first and that she should bring her son Rowan with her. If she had put herself first, as Dermid said she always did, she would have stayed in Ottawa and she would have filed a suit for divorce long ago. Separation from Dermid had achieved nothing. He was just as aggravating and tormenting as he had always been. Just as dangerously attractive to her too, she admitted grudgingly, giving him a sideways glance.

But he wasn't there. He was walking away from her towards the exit doors and Rowan was with him. They were hand in hand and Rowan was occasionally gave a little skip as if he were quite happy to go with a man who, although he was the child's father, was virtually a stranger to him.

Through the door they went and Ellen came to life. Moving as quickly as her swollen feet would allow her, she went after them. Outside the raw damp air sliced through the velvet suit, chilling her body. The wind tweaked at her short curling brown hair, icy drops of rain stung her cheeks and she wished she hadn't packed her raincoat; rain would ruin the velvet suit.

In the next instant the ruin of her suit was forgotten as she realised that Rowan, urged by Dermid, had disappeared into the back of a sleek black car parked by the kerb. It was like seeing her child kidnapped right under her nose.

'Rowan, come back! Dermid, you can't do this!'

'Can't I?' He slid back the cuff of his shirt of cream silk which just showed below the edge of his jacket sleeve and glanced at his watch. 'With a bit of luck we'll catch the only ferry which goes to Portcullin today. Like to change your mind and come with us? Or are you still hankering on driving there ... by yourself, of course.'

She glared up at his mocking face, searching her mind desperately for some sharp rejoinder. But none came to her. Instead she found herself thinking again how good-looking he was.

'Mummy, hurry up!' Rowan's bright head appeared in the doorway of the car. 'I wanna go on a boat, to the castle. Come on!'

'Oh, all right,' she muttered ungraciously, and stepped forward to the car.

'What about your luggage?' Dermid reminded her. 'Going to leave it here?'

'Oh, hell!' Giving him another glare, she turned on her heel and went back into the building. A few minutes later she managed to drag the trolley full of cases out through the exit doors. Dermid was already sitting in the back seat of the car talking to Rowan and it was the driver of the car who put the luggage in the boot for her.

It was a company car, she noticed, as ignoring the space Dermid had left for her in the back seat she slid into the seat next to the driver's; the company being Craig & Rose, spinners of cotton and nylon thread. A Robert Craig had started the business back in the nineteenth century and since then it had grown and grown so that now there was a Craig & Rose factory in some Commonwealth countries and affiliates in some South American and developing African countries too.

Ellen tilted her head back against the head-rest and willed herself to relax as the car swept along the road towards Irvine. She had forgotten how narrow the roads were and how small everything was after Canada. Flat fields, where potatoes were still being harvested stretched away on either side of the road and there were still some leaves clinging to the tidy hawthorn hedges which were spangled with red hawberries and rose-hips. Rowan trees, set in the corners of the fields to frighten hobgoblins and witches away, were as tawny gold as her Rowan's hair and their clusters of orange-scarlet berries swung in the wind.

Her mother had been a Rose before she had married Don Lister, a Canadian Air Force pilot who had been stationed in Scotland at the end of the Second World

War, and she had gone with him, like so many other British women had gone at that time with their Canadian husbands, when he had returned to Canada after the end of the war. War brides, they had been called.

Ellen sighed, thinking of her mother. Janet Lister had been particularly proud of her connections with the wealthy Rose family, long-time partners of the Craigs in the textile business, so he had insisted that Ellen should visit her Rose relatives on her first visit to Britain five years ago.

Twenty years of age, very impressionable and wildly excited by her discovery of her Scottish 'roots', Ellen had enjoyed her stay with various Rose cousins, and it was at the home of one of them that she had met Dermid Craig, dark-eyed and russet-haired and just seven years older than her.

One look at him and she had fallen in love, for with his hawk-like profile, dark red hair and tall rangy figure he had seemed to her to be the embodiment of all the fiercely proud clan chieftains she had read about in the historical romances about Scotland which her mother owned.

But he wasn't a clan chieftain, he had assured her, his eyes glinting with amusement at her suggestion; he was a textile technologist and held a degree to prove that he was, although he did hope one day to be the managing director of Craig & Rose. Ambitious, forceful and very knowledgeable about the business he worked in and also about managing people, he had soon reduced her to submissiveness, thought Ellen with another sigh, so that when he had said he would like to marry her she had agreed without hesitation, too much in love to give a thought to the future or what marriage would involve.

But then if Janet Lister had been able to see into the

future would she had been so keen for her to visit her Rose cousins? wondered Ellen drowsily, her eyelids drooping over her eyes as the warmth of the car and the murmur of Dermid's voice as he talked to Rowan in the back of the car lulled her. If Janet Lister had known that her youngest child and one and only daughter would meet, fall in love with and marry in the short time-space of three weeks the son of Maxwell Craig, a man whom Janet had despised, would she have insisted that Ellen visit the Rose family? Ellen doubted it.

Her head slid sideways and she dozed. When she opened her eyes the road was curving beside a sandy, rock-strewn beach. Surprisingly the clouds were lifting and a watery sunlight was shafting down to dapple the wind-tossed waves of the Clyde Estuary, turning them from dull grey to silvery violet. Across the sea she could see land looming high, the island of Arran all sharp angles and peaks. More islands appeared—the Cumbraes, low-lying like half-submerged green whales, and beyond them the slopes of Bute.

By the time the car turned off the main coast road and nosed its way down a long pier the sun was shining mellowly out of a sky of pale October blue. Across the scintillating turquoise water, showing first sunlit mauve and then shadowed black as puffy white clouds chased above them, the distant hills of Kintyre beckoned temptingly, inviting her to go there, to wander along its shimmering sands, to listen to the sound of its sea and the whisper of the wind in its trees, to linger there in peace, to dream again.

Standing on the top deck of the ferry, gazing out at those hills, Ellen felt the unaccustomed tears of nostalgia prick her eyes and she shivered a little in the cool breeze.

'It's cold up here,' she said abruptly, turning away

from the rail. 'Let's go down to the lower deck and sit in the saloon, Rowan.'

'I wanna stay here,' he objected, wrenching his hand free of hers.

'Haven't you brought a coat with you?' asked Dermid sharply, his eyes flicking over the pinched paleness of her face.

'Yes, I have, but it's in one of my cases,' she muttered, avoiding his glance. Did he remember as she did, quite unexpectedly, that he had asked exactly the same question, five years ago on this top deck of this same ferry? It had been the same time of the year when, only two weeks married, he had taken her to Inchcullin House to meet his grandfather. Then he had taken off the tartan-lined duffle coat he had been wearing and had draped it about her, pulling the hood up over her head, then framing her face with his hands and kissing her. Now, he gave her a narrowed wary glance and didn't offer to take off the sheepskin-lined suede coat he was wearing over his suit. But perhaps he was feeling the cold himself. He did look a little blue around the cheeks.

'You go down below, then,' he ordered. 'I'll stay up here and keep an eye on Rowan.'

She hesitated, suddenly suspicious of his motives. She wouldn't be at all surprised if he made the most of every opportunity to win Rowan away from her.

'Rowan, you look cold too. Come down below with Mummy,' she said, taking his hand in hers again. 'It will be warmer down there and you can have a drink and perhaps some nice cookies.'

'Don't wanna drink, don't want cookies. Wanna stay up here with him!' Again Rowan wrenched his hand free of hers and whirling suddenly, scampered away across the deck. Unused to the rolling motion of the ferryboat as it plunged up and down over the waves, he tottered, lost balance and slid uncontrollably towards the railings.

'Rowan!' shrieked Ellen, diving forward, imagining his small slight body hurtling between the space between the deck and the lower rung of the railing, falling over and over into the churned-up water, to sink below the waves to be seen no more. But Dermid, moving faster than she, reached Rowan before her and swung him up into his arms, then up to his shoulders, where the boy sat with one hand buried in the thickness of his father's hair and smiled down at her triumphantly.

'After that little scare I think it's you who needs the drink, a good strong dram of whisky. The bar should be opening now we've left the shore,' drawled Dermid.

'It's too early in the day for whisky,' she protested, following him down the companionway to the lower deck. 'Besides, we can't take Rowan into the bar.'

'All right, you go and sit in the saloon with him and I'll bring the whisky to you,' he replied equably.

In the comfortable saloon at the stern of the boat Ellen sat near the window so that Rowan could look out. She had managed to buy him a glass of orange juice and couple of Jacobs' Chocolate Club biscuits and a cup of coffee for herself as she doubted if Dermid would be able to bring whisky into the saloon.

It was a while before he reappeared and she was beginning to think that he had decided to stay in the bar when he came through the door carrying two glasses, one in either hand. He set them down on the table and sat down opposite to her.

He sipped his whisky and she fiddled with the glass of amber-coloured liquid he had brought for her, watching the bubbles of the ginger ale which had been added to the whisky and bursting, searching her mind for something to say.

'I ... I ... didn't expect you to meet me,' she muttered suddenly. 'I thought perhaps you'd still be at Inchcullin House.'

'The funeral took place on Tuesday of last week. I returned to Kilruddock the next day,' he replied quietly. Kilruddock was the town where the Craig & Rose head offices and factory were situated. It was also the location of the house he owned and in which they had lived during the first year of their marriage.

'I'm sorry I couldn't attend the funeral,' Ellen said stiffly.

'You weren't expected.'

'And I really don't understand why I have to be present at the reading of your grandfather's will,' she went on. 'After all, I hardly knew him and I'm not a Craig....'

'No, you're not, but Rowan is,' he interrupted her coldly. 'And it's on his account that you've been asked to come in compliance with my grandfather's last wishes.'

'It's very inconvenient for me to be away from Ottawa right now,' she complained.

'Oh, I can imagine,' he jeered. 'Did Walt Stewart threaten to find someone else to do your job when you asked for time off?'

'Well, it wasn't easy,' she muttered. He had come very close to the mark and she could hear Walter Stewart's voice crackling in her ears now. 'Okay,' he had said. 'Take a week, but that's all, and if you're not back by next Monday, forget it. You've been doing a poor job lately ... seem to have lost all that vitality you once had ... so I'm going to give you a piece of advice.

While you're over there sort out your marital affairs, will you? Get a divorce.'

'But ... but ... I'm not sure I want one,' she had protested.

'Well, this separation business isn't doing you any good. That guy is on your mind, I can tell, and you've got to make up your mind sooner or later what it is you want, him or a career. Looks like you can't have both.' He had leaned forward and had added in a lower tone, 'Believe me, Ellen, a clean break is best. I've been through it, so I know. Hanging on to a dream in the hopes of reviving it is just a lot of romantic hogwash.'

On the plane coming over she had thought about Walter's advice and had admitted to herself that he was right. At some time during the next few days she would have to come to a decision. Make a clean break with Dermid or...? She looked across at him. He was just lowering his glass, having emptied it, and his eyes, dark and enigmatic, so alien in his fair-skinned face, met hers.

'It's only for Rowan's sake that I've come,' she said. 'Is that clear?'

'Meaning you haven't come for my sake?' he retorted dryly. 'Oh yes, that's very clear.' He pushed to his feet and held out his free hand for her glass. 'Like a refill?'

'No, no, thank you. I haven't finished this yet, but don't let me stop you from going and getting another drink for yourself.'

'I won't.' His grin mocked her and he left the saloon. Ellen watched him go, feeling the old hot resentment at being left behind boil up unexpectedly within her. It was the story of her marriage to him, she thought bitterly, as she slumped back against the vinyl-covered cushioned seat which she and Rowan were sharing and sipped more whisky and ginger, shuddering a little over its taste.

Dermid had always had some reason for going away that first year they had been married, and even now she could remember very clearly the first time when, nearly three months after they had been married, he had told her that he was being sent by the company to help with the commissioning of the machinery in a new spinning mill which had been set up in India.

'When do we leave?' she had asked, excited by the idea of going to live for a while in a foreign exotic place.

They had been sitting together as they had often sat after the evening meal was over on the big chesterfield in the long wide living room which she had taken so much pleasure in furnishing, and since they had been still very much in love they had sat closely, her head on his shoulder, his arm about her, his hand at her waist.

'I leave, you don't,' he had said softly, and had slid the fingers of his hand under the waistband of her long evening skirt. The tips of them had slithered on the smooth nylon satin of her underslip as he had stroked her stomach. 'Have you forgotten you're pregnant?' he had added.

'No, I haven't,' she had retorted. 'How could I forget when I've been as sick as a dog every morning for nearly three months now?'

'The sickness will pass soon and you'll begin to feel great,' he had murmured, and his lips had been warm against the side of her throat.

'How do you know I will?' she had teased, ruffling his thick hair. 'Have you had a pregnant wife before?'

'No, but I've been reading those books about having babies you've been getting from the library. I hope it's a boy, Ellen.'

'I hope so, too,' she had replied, turning her face to his so that their lips had met and for a while the only talk had been love-talk as the passion on which their relationship had been based had erupted between them and everything else had been forgotten temporarily, swept from their minds by the sensual pleasure they had both derived from satisfying each other's physical desires.

But later as she had lain beside him in bed and had watched the moonlight quivering on the ceiling of their bedroom she had remembered what he had said: 'I leave, you don't,' and she had imagined what being without him would be like and she hadn't been able to bear it in silence.

'You can't go without me, you can't. I won't let you,' she had cried stormily. 'Oh, Dermid, I'll die without you!'

'No, you won't, you'll be fine,' he had murmured reassuringly, and gathering her against him he had stroked her back soothingly, pressing her close to his warm bare tensile body. 'And I'll be back,' he had whispered, his breath tickling her ear. 'It's only for six months. I'll be back for the birth of the baby, I promise you. I'll fly back as soon as it's due. I want to be with you when you're in labour. I want to help you, see our child being born....'

'Six months?' It had seemed like eternity to her. 'But what am I going to do all that time, cooped up in this town? I'll ... I'll go crazy with boredom!'

'You can visit your cousins in Ayr, and you and Molly MacIntyre seem to get on well together and you'll be busy making things for the baby, going to ante-natal classes. There'll be plenty for you to do. You won't be bored,' he had drawled sleepily.

'But it won't be the same without you here,' she had

whispered desperately. Then, knowing he was falling asleep, she had wound her arms about him and had pressed herself against him fiercely. 'Dermid, don't go. Let them send someone else. Stay with me.'

He had stiffened and had moved away from her, unclasping her arms from round his neck and turning on to his back. In the moonlight his clear-cut features had looked as if they had been carved from marble, cold and hard.

'I want to go. It's a job I want to do. It's all part of the experience I need if I'm going to manage the company one day.'

'You want to do it more than you want to stay with me?' She had been hurt and incredulous.

'Ellen, that isn't a fair question,' he had argued. 'I don't want to leave you any more than you want to stay behind, but it's better for your health if you stay here and you'll get proper medical care, the sort you should have while you're carrying a baby.'

'If you love me, really love me, you won't go,' she had protested, too hurt and young to see what he was thinking of her welfare.

'And if you love me you won't make such a bloody fuss about it,' he had retorted in sudden exasperation and heaving over on to his side so that his back was to her and he had taken all the bedclothes with him. 'Now go to sleep,' he had growled. 'I have to be up early in the morning, even if you don't.'

The feel of something wet seeping down her leg brought Ellen back from the past to the present to see with dismay that her glass had tilted over so that the liquor in it had dripped on to her lap and had seeped through her velvet skirt. With a muttered expletive she opened her handbag and took out a tissue to mop up the mess. It would stain the velvet, she was sure it would. She glanced at Rowan. No wonder he was quiet, she thought with a rueful grin. He had started on another chocolate biscuit and she hadn't even heard him ask if he could have it. It would be best not to disturb him by taking it from him and wiping the smears off his face. She could do that later when he had finished eating.

'Myself when young,' Dermid had said at the airport when he had noticed Rowan, and she guessed he had been right, that he had looked something like Rowan when he had been nearly four years of age, had possessed the same stubborn determination to get his own way. How delighted he had been when Rowan had been born. But he had been upset too because she had had a difficult time in labour. Could she ever forget his tenderness towards her afterwards, his care for her in the weeks after the baby had been born.

It had taken her a long time to recover and at the routine six-weekly post-natal check-up the doctor had advised her not to be in too much of a hurry to have another baby, and that same day Dermid had told her that he had to go back to the mill in India because there were still some problems to be solved in the starting up of the machinery.

'But it won't be long before I'm back,' he had comforted her. 'Five weeks at the outside. You'll hardly miss me, you'll be so busy being a mother.'

It was then she had thought of the letter she had received from her parents suggesting that she go and spend some time with them in Canada.

'While you're away, I think I'll go home,' she had said.

'Home? Isn't this home?' Dermid had gestured with one hand to the living room and its furniture.

'I ... I ... meant Ottawa,' she had corrected herself

quickly. 'Dermid, if I go, will you come over there when you return from India? It's time you met Mother and Dad....'

'Past time,' he had replied, his mouth curling ironically. 'I could be wrong, but I have this impression they didn't approve when you married me.'

'That was because we married in such a hurry without waiting for them to come to Scotland to be present when we exchanged vows,' she had explained hurriedly and defensively. Her parents' cool reaction to her excited transatlantic telephone call telling them that she had married Dermid in a brief and joyous civil ceremony before a Scottish registrar had hurt and bewildered her at the time. 'If we could have waited or if we could have gone to Ottawa to be married they might have felt differently about it.'

'Could you have waited?' he had asked, leaning towards her with his mouth slanting in a taunting smile as his glance had gone suggestively to her mouth and his hand had slid possessively upwards from her waist, the long hard fingers fanning out over the fullness of her breast. 'You know you couldn't, and neither could I,' he had whispered. 'You were as ripe as a berry ready for picking and I was eager to reap the harvest, so your parents should be glad we waited long enough to get married first.' And his mouth had closed over hers in a crushing passionate kiss which had expressed all his pent-up hunger for her.

But instead of responding she had stiffened against him as a new fear had rippled through her, the fear of becoming pregnant again so soon after the pain and sickness of that first pregnancy. Pushing against the weight of him, she had managed to wrench her mouth free of his.

'No, not now, not yet,' she had whispered. 'The

doctor said I must be careful, that I shouldn't be in too much of a hurry to conceive again. He said I should talk about it with you, that we should be in agreement on any precautions we should take.'

'I was only kissing you, darling,' Dermid had mocked, rubbing the end of his nose against her cheek. 'You're hardly likely to get pregnant that way.'

'I know that, but when you kiss me it's so hard not to ... oh, don't, Dermid, please move away. Please don't kiss me and touch me like that.' She had blurted it out and in defending her own vulnerability where he was concerned she had been careless of his feelings, just hadn't known how much she might hurt him.

He had moved away from her and had gone with a deliberation which had mocked her right to the other end of the long couch.

'Like that, you mean?' his voice had rasped sarcastically. 'Is that far enough away, or would you like me to go right out of the house?'

'Oh, Dermid,' she had tried to laugh, 'don't be silly. Try to understand....'

'I do understand. I understand very well,' he had interrupted harshly. 'You don't want me near you because I might make you pregnant. Well, after tonight you'll have nothing to worry about for five whole weeks because the distance between us will be much greater, several thousand miles in fact, since I'll be in India and you'll be in Ottawa. And the precautions the doctor talked about won't be necessary.'

Still feeling weak, wanting the comfort she knew only too well he could offer her yet instinctively afraid of her own reactions to that comfort, Ellen had burst into tears and springing to her feet had rushed up to the bedroom.

She hadn't wept for long and she had kept one ear cocked, listening for the quiet opening of the bedroom door, sure that he would come and lie down beside her to gather her into his arms, to whisper that he was sorry he had spoken so callously. But he hadn't come, and eventually she had rolled off the bed and had gone downstairs again to the living room to offer her apologies to him and make everything right between them again. He hadn't been in there. He hadn't been anywhere else in the house either, and for a few minutes she had experienced a terrible and devastating panic, believing he had left her. Then common sense had asserted itself. All his clothing was still in the bedroom. He would hardly have left without taking some of it with him.

Hearing the baby whimper, she had gone back upstairs, had fed him, changed him and put him down to sleep again, then she had bathed and dressed in a new nightgown and had gone to bed. She had fallen asleep almost immediately and hadn't wakened until dawn light when she had heard Rowan crying for his first feed of the day. She had been alone in the bed and the smoothness of the pillow beside her and the flat tidiness of the bedclothes had indicated that Dermid hadn't slept with her.

Trying not to feel disturbed, she had fed Rowan, put him down in his cot and had gone back to the bedroom. To her surprise Dermid had been there fully dressed and he had been packing a suitcase. He had glanced up at her when she went in.

'Rowan all right?' he had asked.

'Yes.' She had gone to sit on the end of the bed. 'Dermid,' she had begun hesitantly, worried by the hard set of his face and the remoteness of his glance, 'where did you go last night?'

'Out,' he had replied briefly, and had begun to zip up his case.

'Where?'

'Does it matter?'

'Yes, I think it does. I ... I ... was worried when I found you weren't in.'

'I went to see a friend,' he had replied brusquely.

'May I know who the friend was?' she had asked, and in spite of herself her voice had trembled.

'If I told you, you wouldn't be any the wiser,' he had said, shrugging into his suit jacket, and had gone to the dressing table to straighten his tie. He had seen her watching his reflection and his eyes had met hers in the mirror and his mouth had quirked at one corner. 'Oh, don't look so upset, Ellen, I didn't sleep out.'

'Then where did you sleep?' She had been unable to keep the jealousy which had been writhing within her from showing in the tone of her voice.

'In the spare bedroom, where else?' The lift of his eyebrows had derided her.

'Dermid, I ... I ... I'm sorry,' she had muttered. 'When I said I didn't want you to touch me I didn't mean that I didn't want to sleep in the same bed as you....'

He had turned to her then, had come across to sit beside her on the edge of the bed. Freshly showered and shaved, his shirt and suit immaculate, his hair a dark flame in the greyness of early morning light, he had been a warm and vigorous presence in the room and she had longed to fling herself against him and plead with him not to leave her again, but something cold and enigmatic in the glinting darkness of his eyes had frozen her to immobility.

'I couldn't come and sleep with you in this bed last night and remain apart from you,' he had said in a low voice. 'I just couldn't. I....' He had broken off and risen to his feet, turning away from her. 'I have to go now,' he had added, picking up his case. 'Write to me and let me know when you're going to Canada. Take what you want in the way of money out of the account.'

He had gone towards the door and almost tripping over the hem of her too long, too wide nightdress, Ellen had run after him. At the top of the stairs he had turned to her. His face had been pale and a muscle had ticked in his cheek as if he had been gritting his teeth.

'Dermid, you will come to Ottawa? Please!' she had whispered, going up to him and half raising her hand as if to touch his face, then letting it drop to her side again.

'I might. It will depend on how long you decide to stay there, won't it?'

'But...'

'There isn't time now,' he had interrupted her gruffly. 'Write to me and tell me your plans.' He had bent his head and had kissed her on the cheek. ' 'Bye, love,' he had muttered, and had gone down the stairs.

'Mummy ... Mummee!' Rowan's voice, strident with distress, his hand pulling at her arm, brought Ellen back from the house in Kilruddock to the saloon of the ferryboat, the persistent hum of diesel engines, the swishing sound of the sea washing against the hull of the boat and the sight of Rowan's face, greenish-white beneath smears of chocolate. 'Mummy, I think I'm going to be sick!' he wailed.

'Oh, no!' Ellen groaned, and looked out of the window. The weather in typical west coast of Scotland fashion had changed again. A squall had blown up, and the wind was churning up the sea so that the boat, now out in the widest part of the estuary, was wallowing from wave to wave in a way that was distinctly sick-making.

'Not here, Rowan, please,' she begged, getting to her feet. Staggering a little as the deck heaved beneath her feet, she looked round the saloon. There were more people in it now. Presumably they had come below to shelter from the wind. But Dermid wasn't among them. Her lips tightened. He had made it very clear that he preferred to sit and drink in the bar rather than keep her and Rowan company.

Rowan made a horrible gurgling sound and at once she grabbed his hand to pull him in the direction of the door. Lurching along in the passageway, she searched vainly for a sign indicating where the toilets were.

'Can I help you, missus?' A member of the crew, a steward judging by his uniform, was coming towards her.

'My little boy feels sick. He's not used to the sea.' Neither am I, she thought wildly as her own stomach heaved.

The man nodded understandingly and opened one of the narrow doors beside him.

'Here you are, missus, you take him in there. You can lie down if you want on the bunk. It'll be a wee while yet before we get to harbour and the weather will get worse before it gets better, I shouldn't wonder.'

Pushing Rowan before her, Ellen went into the narrow cabin. Rowan was sick in the wash-basin and cried when he had finished vomiting. She managed to clean him up with the face-cloth and towel provided and lifting him on to the lower bunk she lay down beside him, holding him closely, stroking his red-gold hair until gradually his sobs stopped, his eyelids drooped and he slept.

He was a beautiful child, she thought, as she gazed

dreamily at his slightly flushed tear-stained cheeks and long dark lashes. A child born of love, for they had been in love, she and Dermid, intensely and passionately in love six years ago.

Then what had happened to them? Why had they become separated? Was it her fault or his? No, they were both responsible for the tug-of-war their marriage had become, with both of them pulling in opposite directions, each of them refusing to give in to the other.

Oh God, she was tired of thinking about it, tired of trying to find out how she could have done things differently, tired of trying to hang on to a dream. Tired, tired, tired. If only she could sleep and never wake up again!

Slowly her eyelids drooped too. The night without sleep and the tension which had built up in her since meeting Dermid again had made inroads into her nervous system. Exhausted, she fell asleep, one arm flung protectively over her child.

CHAPTER TWO

ELLEN became slowly aware that the ferryboat was no longer rolling and that the chug-chug of the engines had died down to a slow consistent hum. Feeling cold and stiff, she lay for a few moments with her eyes closed wondering what had happened, then knuckles rapped sharply on the door. Opening her eyes, she saw Rowan's head bright as a new penny. He was still asleep, his head heavy against her arm. Knuckles rapped again on the door, more imperatively, and she moved, sliding her arm beneath Rowan. Swinging off the bed, she went to the door and opened it. The steward stood there, his bright Celtic blue eyes peering at her curiously.

'We're at Portcullin, missus, as far as we go,' he said. 'Is the wee lad feeling better now?'

'Yes, thank you. He's asleep.'

'Do you have any luggage to take ashore?' he asked.

'Er ... yes.' Ellen pushed her hair back from her brow. Drowsiness was still clogging her mind. She felt as if she had slept for a hundred years. 'I think Derm ... I mean my husband is taking care of it,' she mumbled.

'Just so, just so,' said the steward. 'Then I'll help you with the lad.' He stepped past her into the cabin and looked down at Rowan. 'It seems a pity to wake him, so it does. Your only bairn, missus?' Ellen nodded and he went on chattily, 'I have four meself. They keep the wife busy.' He lifted Rowan easily in his arms. 'You lead the way, missus. Turn to the right along the passage and you'll come to the gangway.'

There was only time to step into her shoes and grab her handbag. No time to study her appearance in the small mirror, comb her hair or attend to her make-up. No time to pick the bits of fluff and lint off her velvet suit, no time to try and smooth its creases. She had to face Dermid's curious probing gaze looking a mess again.

The mocking cackle of seagulls hovering above the warm currents of air which issued from the ferryboat's funnel greeted her as she stepped from the passageway towards the gangway which slanted down to the quayside. The squall had passed over and the sun was shining again out of a blue sky across which puffy white clouds were racing. It shone on the white walls and red trim of the buildings on the sturdy stone quayside to which the ferry-boat was tied up and glittered on the two vehicles which were parked near them.

She recognised one of those vehicles at once. Sleek and silvery, it was the Rolls-Royce which had belonged to Dermid's grandfather, and James Blair, his chauffeur and gardener, was putting her cases in the boot. Then where was Dermid? She didn't have to look far to find him. He was standing by the other smaller car with a tall well-built woman who was wearing an elegant suit and whose short smooth hair gleamed silvery-yellow in the sunlight. Dermid seemed to be very interested in what she was saying to him and didn't look round as Ellen stepped off the gangway.

Ignoring him, she went straight across to James Blair and the steward followed her, still carrying Rowan. James Blair's normally morose face creased into a welcoming smile and he lifted his peaked cap to her as she approached him.

'Good day to ye, Mrs Craig,' he said in his lilting Scottish voice.

'How are you, James?' She held out her hand to him and he took it rather hesitantly in his as if he wasn't sure he was supposed to shake hands with her.

'Ach, I'm fine, just fine, Mrs Craig—and how's ye-self?'

'Well, thank you.'

'Mummy,' Rowan sounded anxious as he came awake in the steward's arms. 'Where are we, Mummy? Where's the boat?'

'We've arrived, darling.' She turned to smile at the steward and thank him as he let Rowan slide to the ground, but her glance went past him to Dermid who was still with the fair-haired woman. Who was the woman? And why was he paying so much attention to her? She felt a familiar stirring of jealousy and squashed it immediately. The steward walked off towards the ferry and James Blair suggested she and Rowan should get in the car as he swung the door open for her politely.

'Come on, Rowan,' she urged. 'In you go. Isn't this a lovely car?'

'Don't wanna be in a car. Wanna be on a boat,' complained Rowan stubbornly and contrarily, refusing to move. 'Wanna be with him,' he added, suddenly spotting Dermid and, dodging round her, he took off across the sunlit stones of the quayside.

'Rowan, Rowan, come back at once!' The wind, which was pulling at her hair and blowing it into her eyes, took Ellen's words and tossed them away in the wrong direction. Biting her lower lip in annoyance, she watched Rowan run up to Dermid, lifting his arms to him. At once Dermid stooped and swung the boy on to his shoulders as he had done on the boat. But instead of turning and coming across to the car he went on standing by the other woman, not talking to her but obviously listening very intently to what she was saying.

'I'm thinking the dinner Bessie has been preparing for ye all morning will be spoilt if we have to wait much longer.' James Blair's voice was softly rebuking and after a quick glance at him which noted that he was watching the group standing by the other car Ellen looked at her watch. It was twenty-five after twelve and she had forgotten it was Sunday. She had forgotten too that dinner at Inchcullin was always served in the middle of the day, a wholesome but sometimes stodgy meal designed to sustain you through the rest of the day.

'I'll go and tell Dermid to come,' she muttered, and walked purposefully across the quayside. Reaching his side, she spoke abruptly and jerkily, knowing she was being rude by interrupting the other woman but not caring because she felt she had the right to demand Dermid's attention.

'James says dinner will be spoilt if we don't go to Inchcullin House right now,' she said.

The other woman's voice stopped. From under her eyebrows Ellen gave her a quick assessing look, noting the fine-skinned, angular face and deep blue eyes under haughtily arched eyebrows; a beautiful woman with a shapely figure set off by the close-fitting lambswool sweater she was wearing under the jacket of her bluish-grey tweed suit; a woman of about forty-five years of age, experienced and sophisticated.

'I'll be with you in a minute.' Dermid's voice was cold and authoritative as he set Rowan down on the ground. 'Go with your mother, lad,' he ordered curtly, and his eyes were nearly black as he flashed an irritated glance at Ellen. 'You were saying, Ann?' he went on courteously as he turned back to the other woman.

Her cheeks flaming with colour, Ellen turned sharply on her heel, feeling Rowan's hot sticky fingers pushing into her hand. How dared Dermid treat her as if she were of no account! How dared he snub her like that in front of another woman? Behind her she heard a car door slam, then the roar of an engine starting up. In a few seconds Dermid was beside her, his footsteps sounding crisp and clear on the granite blocks of the quayside and his shadow slanting sideways to merge with hers and Rowan's.

'Did you have to be so rude?' he snapped tensely between his teeth. 'Couldn't you have waited until Ann had finished speaking before you spoke?'

'The way she was going on I could have been waiting for ever,' she retorted shakily. 'And apparently what she had to say was of far more absorbing interest to you than Rowan and I am.'

His hand gripped her arm painfully, hard fingers biting through the soft velvet and silk to the flesh and bone beneath, making her wince as he swung her round to face him.

'Listen, you jealous little bitch,' he grated. 'Ann is an old friend of....'

'Oh, I could see that,' she jibed waspishly, interrupting him. 'She is *old*. Older than you by about twelve years, I would guess. But that's the latest trend, right now, isn't it? Older women getting together with younger guys.'

'Shut up!' he hissed, his eyes flashing angrily. 'Ellen, what is the matter with you?'

'Nothing, nothing at all,' she replied, tossing her hair back out of her eyes. 'I'm just saying what I think, giving my opinion—I'm entitled to do that, I believe. I suppose you met her in the bar, your *old* friend,' she went on more stormily, her voice breaking a little. 'I suppose she was there when you went to get that first drink and that's why you went back there for another drink. You preferred to stay and drink with her rather than be with Rowan and me.'

'Can you honestly say you encouraged me to stay with you?' he retorted harshly. 'Oh, no, quite the reverse. You wanted me to leave you because being with me makes you uncomfortable, doesn't it? Sure I went back to the bar and stayed there, but not because Ann was there. I didn't come across her until I was looking for you after that squall blew up. I searched the whole bloody boat for you. Where did you get to?'

'Rowan was sick and I felt a bit queasy too. The steward let us go into a cabin and lie down,' she mumbled.

'Are you all right now?' The red sparks of anger which had flickered in the dark depths of his eyes had gone out. Warmly brown in the sunlight, his glance drifted over her face before slanting down to Rowan who was surprisingly placid for once, swinging on her hand and sucking his thumb while he stared at some rubbish which was being blown about by the wind.

'As if you cared,' Ellen taunted, still upset by his treatment of her in front of the woman called Ann.

'God, you have one hell of a temper,' Dermid rasped, his fingers tightening on her arm. 'I've a good mind to. . . .'

'To shake me?' she flung at him. 'Go on, go ahead, do it. Shake me here in front of James Blair, give him a fine tale to carry to Bessie who'll report it to your Aunt Agnes, who will know then that your relationship isn't as cosy and as comfortable as I expect you've led her and everyone else in your family to believe.'

'I haven't led Agnes to believe anything,' he retorted,

his face stiffening with pride. 'Unlike you I've never discussed our relationship with her or anyone else. They can believe what the hell they like. The way you and I choose to live is none of their damned business.'

'Dermid, watch your language, please. Think of the child,' she whispered fiercely, trying to pull her arm free of his grasp. 'And you've got a grip like a vice, do you know that? My arm will be black and blue with bruises when you've finished with it. *Ah*, let go, please!' she cried as his fingers tightened remorselessly. 'You must have drunk a lot of Scotch in the bar to make you behave like this. You used not to be a wife-beater.'

'Where did you learn to be so bitchy, Ellen?' he demanded threateningly, his face so close to hers that she could smell the liquor on his breath and could see the dangerous gleam in his narrowed eyes. 'From your mother? Or from the people you work with?' He let go of her so suddenly that she staggered a little. 'Come to think of it,' he went on tauntingly, thrusting his hands into his trouser pockets and rocking back and forth on his heels while his glance raked her insolently, 'that's what I should have done years ago—beaten you.'

'I'd have hated you if you had. I'd have left you,' she stormed.

'So where's the difference?' he mocked. 'You hate me now. For what?'

'I don't. Oh, you....' About to call him names, she broke off, remembering Rowan. Turning away, she went towards the Rolls, pulling the child after her. Once again James Blair swung open the rear door for her. She got in first and slid along the wide seat to the far corner. Rowan climbed up beside her and still sucking his thumb leaned against her. Ellen hoped that Dermid would sit in front with James, but when she looked round she found he was sitting down in the other corner and James was shutting the door after him.

The big grey car purred arrogantly past the fishermen's wharf, past piles of fish boxes, nets and buoys, past the green, black and varnished fishing boats which, bobbing on the wind-ruffled water of the harbour, were tugging vainly at the strong rope warps tying them to the iron bollards. Leaving the wharf behind, the car turned up the main street of the town past the closed shops and the hotel. People dressed in Sunday clothes were coming out of church, walking down the flight of grey granite steps, women holding on to hats which the strong wind threatened to whip from their heads, young girls laughing as they tried to hold down their skirts.

On up the hill the car sped smoothly past the sky-pointing dark fingers of stone which were all that remained of the medieval Castle Cullin. Over the brow of the hill the Rolls floated and down the other side towards the sea which glinted turquoise and silver where the sun shone on it and glowered black and purple where clouds shadowed it.

Turning right on to the north-winding coast road, the car took the bumps and dips in it as if they didn't exist. Her head against the smooth velvety interior lining of the car, Ellen felt the tension which the quarrel with Dermid had sent twanging along her nerves easing as she stared out at the view of island-strewn sea. The nearest island, the dark low-lying one, was Gigha, she remembered, and the green one beyond it serenely smiling in the sun was Islay. And what was the name of the one with the three mountains? Unthinkingly she turned to ask Dermid and hesitated, for it looked as if he had gone to sleep, his long legs stretched before him, his head tipped back against the cushioned headrest.

Ellen studied his face. The years they had been apart

had left their marks on him. There were lines beside his mouth which hadn't been there before; lines etched by humour, she didn't doubt, because he had always liked to laugh, but also by something else. Bitterness? Cynicism? And there were glints of silver in the russet-coloured hair which had fallen forward over his brow.

He had always been distinctive, she thought. It had always been easy to pick him out in a crowd, but now he was beginning to look distinguished as well as handsome. He looked what he was, she supposed what he had become over the past few years, a successful, dynamic businessman, confident in his own abilities with a flair for looking elegant no matter what he was wearing and a way of conveying that he looked even better without his clothes.

Ellen's cheeks burned suddenly and unexpectedly and she looked away from him quickly, conscious of tiny nerves in the lower part of her body twisting and fluttering with desires which had been asleep for a long time. Knuckles pressed hard against her mouth, she stared out at the sea again.

How many other women had felt like this after looking at Dermid? How many other women had there been in his life these past three years? She knew of one at least. Dermid wasn't of the stuff of which puritans are made. Self-denial wasn't part of his outlook on life. He was the cavalier type, like his father had been, taking his pleasure where he found it. *Maybe I'll be like him if you don't love me enough,* he had said once to her, and although he had spoken teasingly she had known he had meant it.

When had he said that and why? Oh yes, she remembered only too well. It was all rushing back into her mind to torment her, that memory she had tried so hard to hold back, the memory of the idyllic week they had once spent together at her parents' summer cottage in the Gatineau hills north of Ottawa. Dermid had flown from India to join her there as she had asked him and that week had been a time of enchantment for both of them as they had rediscovered each other in the log cabin among the autumn woods of dark spruce and scarlet-leaved maples, high upon a hill above the dimpling waters of a lake.

It had been there, on the last afternoon, as they had made love among the cushions they had set on the bearskin hearthrug before the crackling blaze of a birch log fire, that he had said to her:

'Whatever happens to come between us, we'll have had this, Ellen. This week has been perfect.'

'What could possibly come between us?' she had murmured out of the lazy, delicious haze of sensuousness which had enveloped her.

'Work, people,' he had replied. He had paused and dark lashes had drifted down over his eyes hiding their expression. 'Your mother doesn't like me,' he had added quietly.

She had known her mother didn't like him, and had discovered why a few days after she had returned to Ottawa from Scotland.

'Why don't you and Dad approve of my marriage to Dermid?' she had blurted out, unable to ignore any longer the coldness which any mention of Dermid was received, particularly by her mother.

'We feel you rushed into marriage too hastily,' Janet Lister had replied slowly, obviously picking her words. 'And that possibly he stamped you into it by ... by ... well, by making love to you too intimately.' Faint colour had stained Janet's cheeks as she had touched on a delicate subject, one she would have preferred not to mention.

'You mean that you believe Dermid seduced me and that's why...?' Ellen had broken off to laugh incredulously. 'Oh, Mother, surely you know I've more sense than to let that happen to me!'

'Sometimes the most sensible of women can be seduced, especially when an attractive and experienced man sets his mind on seducing her,' Janet had said stiffly.

'Then you do think Dermid is attractive?' Ellen had been quick to pick that up.

'As attractive as that red-haired devil Maxwell Craig, his father, was.'

'You knew Maxwell Craig?' Ellen had explained.

'I knew him. He married my second cousin, Barbara Rose. I was a bridesmaid at their wedding, and when I think of the way he treated her later just because she couldn't have any children, how he made her life a misery with his carryings on with that gypsy....'

'You mean Dermid's mother, don't you? Her name is Kate MacKinnon now and she's married to a farmer. I know she's very dark, but I didn't realise she had gypsy blood in her.'

'You've met her? Then he's told you that he's....' Janet had broken off again as she hesitated to call a spade a spade.

'That he was born illegitimately?' Ellen had supplied for her. 'Yes, he has. Dermid and I don't have any secrets from one another,' she had gone on proudly. 'And I think it's a pity that your cousin Barbara didn't have the kindness of heart to divorce Dermid's father when she realised she couldn't become pregnant. Then he could have married Kate and Dermid would have been born legitimately.'

'Oh, it's easy for you to criticise Barbara,' Janet had remarked dryly. 'Wait until it happens to you. Wait until you know what it's like to have the man you've sworn to love and cherish turn away from you to another woman and to have to suffer the indignity of learning that it was to that other woman he was hurrying to be with when he was killed in a car crash and not you. You'll think and feel differently then.'

But to give credit where credit was due, Janet and Don Lister had made Dermid welcome when he had come to Ottawa. They had made a good attempt to disguise their antipathy towards him and had offered to keep Rowan with them for a week while Ellen and Dermid had a week's holiday, and so Ellen had defended her mother when she had replied to Dermid's suggestion that Janet didn't like him.

'It's because she doesn't know you yet,' she had replied soothingly, sitting up on the rug and leaning over him. 'She thinks you might turn out to be like your father.'

She had said it teasingly and had been surprised when his face had hardened and his eyes had narrowed to dangerously gleaming slits as he had pulled her down on top of him.

'Maybe I will be like him if you don't love me enough,' he had drawled threateningly. 'Make love to me now, Ellen,' he had urged her in a whisper. 'Show me that you want me as much as I want you.'

And finding herself for once in a position of dominnance, feeling strange new sensations thrilling through her body, she had shown him there among the cushions while the firelight had flickered over them, burnishing their skins with an orange red glow, adding a new dimension to their lovemaking so that they had reached greater heights of ecstasy than ever before.

Next day their idyll had been rudely interrupted. A cable from Scotland had requested Dermid's immediate return to work and he had left Ottawa without her and Rowan.

'Come back when you feel ready to leave your parents,' he had said to her. 'I realise they miss you when you're away because you're the last of their brood to leave the nest, so give them some more of your time. I'll be away again for a while, probably in Hong Kong where we're installing new machinery, so try to coincide your return to Scotland with mine, some time in early December, and we'll have our first Christmas with Rowan.'

She should have gone with him then. She should never have stayed on in Ottawa, she could see that now. But at the time she hadn't realised that the longer she stayed the more difficult it would become for her to leave. She hadn't known then that her father would have a sudden heart attack and die and that her mother would cling to her in the extremity of her grief because she was the only one of Janet's children who was there on the spot at the time.

Dermid had been fairly understanding and had writen to tell her to stay with Janet until she was more able to cope, and the weeks had slid by and it had been Christmas almost before she had realised it. It had been impossible for her to leave her mother right then, so Dermid had flown to Ottawa to spend the festive season there.

But it had not been a happy time. Janet had shown her resentment of Dermid from the moment he had set foot in her house and by New Year's Eve his mood had been brittle.

'I'm not staying any longer,' he had said to Ellen when they had had a few minutes alone. 'I'm flying back to Scotland today. Are you coming with me?'

'Dermid, there's something I've been wanting to ask

you', she had replied. 'I ... I've been offered a job here and I'd like to take it.'

'What sort of a job?' he had asked slowly.

'It's at the local T.V. studios. One of the producers there is a neighbour of Mother's here and he's asked me if I'd like to do some interviewing on an afternoon show. He thinks I'd be good at it.' Her voice had risen excitedly as she had given him more details. 'It's something I'd like to try, and I might never get the opportunity again.'

'Couldn't you find something like that to do in Scotland?' he had asked.

'No, I don't think so. I mean, I'm not Scottish, am I? And I don't have any contacts in commercial T.V. over there.'

'Did your mother put you up to this?' he had demanded suspiciously.

'No, but she thinks it's a good idea.'

'I bet she does,' he had said dryly. 'And now I know what was behind those little pep talks she's been giving me about how different life is for a woman these days; how she wished you hadn't married before you'd had a chance to feel your independence.' He had given her a darkly glittering glance from under frowning eyebrows. 'She would like you and me to split, do you know that?'

'She wouldn't, I'm sure she wouldn't! She has a great respect for the institution of marriage. And I don't want us to split. I want to stay married to you.' She had gone up to him and had put her arms about him. 'I love you, Dermid, but I'd like to do this job, to find out if I can do it, prove to myself that I'm capable of being more than a wife and a mother.'

'What about Rowan? What will happen to him?'

'He'll be fine. After the first six months a child

doesn't need its mother to be with it all the time. I can leave him with Mother. She's already said she'd love to have him. Or I can find someone else to mind him during the hours I'm not at home,' she had hurried on to say as she had seen his face go taut and sceptical when she had mentioned her mother. 'Oh, you don't understand, do you?' she had sighed when he had turned away from her and had gone over to the living room window to watch the snowflakes floating down outside.

'I'm trying to, God knows I'm trying to,' he had said rather hoarsely. 'You want to be free of me, isn't that what you're saying?'

'Only to do my own thing as you do yours. You do a job you like doing. You go away and leave me behind, so I don't see why I can't do the same.'

'You're bored with being married, isn't that it?' he challenged, swinging round to face her.

'Perhaps. Dermid. Surely we can work something out. Other couples manage to do their work in different places and remain married. You could come and see me here when you can and Rowan and I could come and see you when. . . .'

'No!' The negative had seemed to explode out of him.

'Why not?'

'I don't like half-measures, that's why.' There had been a long silence and she had just been going to give in, to say she would go back to Scotland with him, when he had said abruptly, 'All right, you do your own thing, as you call it. Stay here and take that job. We'll separate for a year.'

'Separate?'

'I believe that's what it's called when a wife and husband don't live together any more.' His voice had been cold, and looking back Ellen realised that it was in that moment his feelings towards her had changed. 'At the end of the year, next Christmas, we'll review the situation,' he had added, and she must have looked stunned because he had made an exclamation of irritation. 'It's the only way, Ellen. I'll get out of your life for a while and you can have your fling at independence if it will make you happy.'

He had left then, had packed his bags and had left her mother's house, and she hadn't seen him again until today.

Slowly she turned her head. Her glance drifted to his legs, long and muscular, shaping the fine tweed of his trousers. Her glance travelled upwards to linger on the big graceful hand which rested casually on one of his knees, then on, up again. His suit jacket was unbuttoned and so was his waistcoat, as if he didn't care for the restraint it imposed upon him, and he had loosened the knot of his tie. Above the crisp collar of his cream shirt the line of his jaw was still taut. In all the lean length of him there was no sign of self-indulgence. In fact she thought his face was too thin, the cheeks a little hollow and gaunt....

Damn, he was looking at her, his eyes slitted, gleaming with a predatory light as if he would like to.... Again she looked away from him quickly, out of the window, forcing herself to concentrate on the view. The road was curving downwards again towards the sea. Ahead a rocky headland jutted out, darkly green against the glittering blue. White spray leapt upwards where waves dashed against rocks.

'I'm hungry,' Rowan announced suddenly. 'I want my lunch. Mummy, I want peanut butter and jelly sandwiches for lunch.'

'Ellen, why haven't you done anything about that lisp?' Dermid spoke sharply and critically.

'I have. The psychiatrist said he'll grow out of it in time, that it's best if we ignore it when he speaks like that. He's only doing it to get attention.'

'A psychiatrist? You took him to see a psychiatrist?' Dermid sat up and glared at her as if she had committed a crime.

'Yes, at the children's hospital. You see, Rowan was having behaviour problems at the day care centre....'

'What the hell is a day care centre?' he interrupted roughly.

'A place where working mothers can leave their children for the day, where a child can be looked after properly, often better than he can be looked after at home. Rowan loves going there because there are other children to play with.'

'If he loves it why does he have behaviour problems?' he asked dryly.

'I don't know. That's why I took him to be assessed by a psychiatrist.'

'And did he tell you why?' The dark brown eyes were derisive now.

'Er ... yes ... well, in a way.' Not for anything was she going to tell him that the psychiatrist had told her to give up work and stay home with Rowan, give him more of her time and attention and if possible end her separation from her husband so that the child would have a chance to know his father and receive his love and attention too. Her ears still burned whenever she recalled the criticism and humiliation of that interview.

'What did the psychiatrist say, Ellen? I've a right to know. Rowan is as much mine as he is yours.' Dermid's voice was daunting.

'One would hardly believe it, considering how you've stayed away from him all this time,' she retorted, and had the satisfaction of seeing him go pale and the mocking glint fade from his eyes.

'I've stayed away from him, as you put it, for one reason only—because he happened to live with you and your mother. Several times I've written to you asking you to bring him to see me. I'd have taken him off your hands, had him live with me for a while....'

'For another woman to look after him?' she flared, and he swore exasperatedly.

'Well, who the hell do you think has been looking after him in Ottawa but other women?'

'At least I've been there every evening to put him to bed and every week-end to take him out. Would you have been, I wonder, if he'd lived with you?' Her voice had risen. Rowan whimpered and Dermid flicked a warning glance at James Blair's stiff shoulders where they rested against the front seat.

'I'm not going to discuss the matter here,' he said softly. 'And not while you're on the verge of hysteria.'

'So I'm hysterical now, am I?' Ellen seethed. 'Then where would you like to discuss the matter? In front of a lawyer, or before the judge in a divorce court?'

For a moment they sat facing each other staring at each over their child's bright head. Then Rowan, sensing trouble, climbed on to Ellen's knee and put his arms about her neck.

'Mummy, don't cry,' he urged her.

'No, don't cry, Ellen,' Dermid mocked. 'I might be tempted to comfort you too—and we both know what will happen if I do.'

She gave him an uncertain glance, but he had turned away to look out of the window. The car was approaching Inchcullin Loch now, following the shoreline round to the head of a deep bay, and she could see the gilded points on the tops of the turrets of the house glinting in the sunlight above the dark pine trees.

Off the road the car turned down a driveway edged by rhododendron bushes. The driveway ended in a wide flagged courtyard in front of the house. Built of grey granite, three storeys high, it had enough gables and turrets to make it an ideal setting for a story of Gothic romance, and at the sight of it Rowan's eyes went round.

'Is this the castle?' he lisped.

'This is the castle,' said Dermid as he got out of the car. Turning back, he held out his hand to help Rowan down and the boy put his hand without hesitation into his father's grasp.

'Do you live here?' he asked, tipping his red-gold head back to look the long way up to Dermid's face.

'No, but my grandfather did, and I used to come here when I was a boy.'

'A boy like me?' persisted Rowan.

'A boy something like you,' replied Dermid. 'I was older than you. . . .' His voice died away to a murmur as he walked across the leaf-strewn courtyard towards the steep steps which led up to the side door of the house.

She should be glad Rowan went with his father so willingly, thought Ellen as she got out of the car and followed them, but she had this deep-seated distrust of Dermid's motives. It would be just like him to go all out to win Rowan away from her, then if they did go through with a divorce he would claim custody of the child, submitting to the judge that she wasn't fit to have care of him because while living with her Rowan had developed a lisp and the tendency to suck his thumb.

The steps loomed up before her and in her anxiety to catch up with Rowan she tripped on the second step, banged her knee sharply on the edge of the third step and groaned as she felt her other stocking snap and ladder. *God*, what a disastrous day this was proving to be! Her velvet suit ruined, her stockings laddered, her feet swollen, her child being slowly and subtly seduced away from her by his father, her nerves twanging and fluttering every time she looked at Dermid or found him looking at her.

By the time she reached the house Bessie Blair, James's wife and housekeeper of Inchcullin House, was standing in the open door holding Rowan in her plump arms and exclaiming over him in admiration while he leaned away from her and stared at her solemnly, blinking his long lashes at her.

'Ach, it's a fine wee bairn ye are, so it is,' Bessie was saying. 'Ye must be proud of him, Mr Craig.'

'He'll do,' Dermid replied laconically, and stepping past Bessie disappeared inside the house.

Bessie's broad shining face beamed at Ellen in welcome.

'Come away in now, Mrs Craig,' she said. 'I'll show you to your room. I'm thinking ye'll be liking to have a wash and to change y'r clothes before ye have y'r dinner. The wee laddie too looks as if a drop of soap and water wouldna' do him any harm.'

'That sounds good, Bessie. Is there time? We were delayed at the pier and James seemed to think the dinner would spoil if we were late,' said Ellen as she stepped into the hallway.

'Ach, ye don't want to be taking any notice of him,' said Bessie tartly. 'It would his own dinner he was thinking of, not yours. Miss Agnes said I was to have it ready for one-thirty, so she did, and it's one-fifteen now, so there's plenty of time.'

The house was just the same, Ellen thought, as she followed Bessie across the hall with its dark panelling on which oil paintings of previous owners hung, its high ceiling edged by intricately-designed plaster carvings of leaves and roses, its shining parquet floor on which Persian rugs were scattered, traps for anyone who walked carelessly. She must remember to warn Rowan about them or he would spend his time skidding on them and landing on his bottom just as she had when she had first stayed in that house.

'How is Miss Craig?' she asked Bessie as they went up the wide staircase. Bessie was still spoiling Rowan by carrying him when he could easily have walked up by himself, and judging by the smug look on his face as he peeped back at her over Bessie's shoulder he was enjoying every minute of being held against Bessie's cushiony bosom.

'She's as well as can be expected under the circumstances,' replied Bessie. 'For all she knew it was coming her father's death was a great shock to her. They'd been together for so long, ye ken.'

'He was a kind old gentleman,' said Ellen. Under her hand the broad mahogany banister was smooth and slippery and she could remember sliding down it five years ago after Dermid, who had shown her the way, and falling into his held-out arms as she had slid off the curve at the end. How young and foolish she had been five years ago, but happy—oh, so very happy.

'Aye, he was kind, none kinder,' breathed Bessie as she went round the bend in the stairway and the sunlight which shafted in through the big stained glass window dappled her and Rowan with blobs of blue, crimson and emerald. 'I mind the day he brought Mr Dermid here for the first time. Not much older than this laddie, he was, but I'm thinking his hair was darker, had more of a touch of brown in it. "This is my grandson, Bessie," Mr Craig said, and he looked that fierce at me as if he expected me to say the lad wasn't. "Yes, sir," I said. "And how long will he be staying?" And he says, "For as long as his mother will let him." He was that grieved, ye see, by the death of Mr Maxwell, his only son, and he'd gone to a lot of trouble to find Mr Dermid's mother and persuade her to let him bring the boy here.'

Bessie came to a stop outside a door on the wide first floor landing and set Rowan down.

'Ach, it's a weight ye are, young feller-me-lad,' she said breathlessly. 'Either that or I'm getting old.' She looked directly at Ellen and her pale blue eyes were reproachful. 'I'm thinking the old man would have loved to have seen this bairn too, his great-grandchild. It's a pity ye couldna' have come to visit him. Ach, but that's the way of the world, now, isn't it? Families all split up and scattered to the four winds.'

She knows, thought Ellen. She knows about Dermid and me. Biting her lip to keep the tears back which had sprung to her eyes in reaction to Bessie's reproach, she followed the woman into the big bedroom. Shiny Victorian-styled mahogany furniture crowded the walls and the bed with its heavy wooden bed ends looked wide enough to sleep six adults quite comfortably. An Indian carpet, patterned in red, yellow and blue, covered the floor and fine lace curtains hung at the two long windows.

'I've put ye in here because it has a grand view of the loch and the sea beyond,' said Bessie, bustling across the room to a door. 'And it has this dressing room opening off it.' She opened the door and beckoned to Ellen. 'I thought the bairn could sleep in here.'

Ellen went across and followed her into the 'wee dressing room', which was actually big enough to be a normal single-sized bedroom in a modern house. It was also furnished with a dressing table and wardrobe and a drop-sided cot of old-fashioned design in which she guessed Dermid had once slept and his father before him, perhaps even his grandfather. It was easily big enough for Rowan, but would he sleep in it? she wondered. He had been sleeping in a small bed for nearly a year now. She glanced at Bessie. The woman was standing watching her, her pale eyes expectant, obviously waiting for her to make some expression of approval.

'It looks very comfortable, Bessie,' she muttered. 'You've gone to a lot of trouble.'

'Ach, it was no trouble....' began Bessie, and broke off as an eerie spine-chilling shriek came from the bedroom. '*Lawks*!' exclaimed the housekeeper. 'Whatever was that?'

'Rowan.' Whirling, Ellen rushed back into the big bedroom and looked round. There was no sign of Rowan, but his frantic shrieks of 'Mummy, Mummy!' and the thudding of sturdy shoes kicking against wood were coming from the huge forbidding-looking Victorian wardrobe which took up most of one wall of the bedroom.

Ellen sprang across to the wardrobe, took hold of the gilt handle on the mirrored door and wrenched it open, holding out her arms just in time to catch Rowan as he hurled himself out of it.

'Mummy, Mummy, there's a big bat in there! It flew right at me and tried to bite me,' he cried, gripping her tightly with his fingers, his eyes squeezed closed as he rested his head on her shoulder, his body shaking from head to foot.

'It was no such thing as a bat, laddie,' said Bessie, laughter rumbling through her voice. 'It was this old hat belonging to *your* granddad, your dad's dad. I must have missed it when I was clearing the clothes out of the cupboard.' She was holding a tweed deerstalker hat with ear-flaps in her hand. 'Look, laddie,' she added, holding it out to show it to him, 'that's all it was.'

Rowan opened his eyes cautiously and looked at the hat and then up at Bessie's twinkling eyes.

'You're sure?' he lisped.

'Aye, I'm sure. There are no bats in this house and none in the wardrobe—but ye'll have to be careful not to get shut in there again, won't you? The door swings closed easily and once you're shut in ye canna get out again. Now, come along with me to the bathroom and I'll give that bonny face of yours a wee lick with a flannel while y'r mum looks for some clean trews and a clean shirt for ye in one of those cases my Jamie has brought up. We canna' have ye going to meet Miss Agnes with chocolate in your hair and down your front, can we? Such pretty hair it is, too.'

'Who's Miss Agnes?' asked Rowan, sliding down from Ellen's arms, his faith in human nature restored again.

'Well now, she's by way of being y'r dad's aunty, which makes her your great-aunty, and she lives in this house.'

'It's not a house, it's a castle,' asserted Rowan. 'Mummy says it is.'

'Castle, then,' replied Bessie patiently, taking his hand and leading him towards the door.

'Is Miss Agnes the dragon?' asked Rowan, and Ellen's mouth twitched in involuntary amusement as the door closed after them. Anyone less like a dragon than the gentle, dreamy-eyed Agnes it would be hard to find, she thought as she went over to the cases James had brought up and had placed on a broad wooden blanket chest at the foot of the bed.

There were four cases, not three, the fourth one being made of tough leather and carrying the tags of several airlines. Dermid's case. Ellen looked round the room. Bessie had assumed that she and Dermid would be sharing a room, in spite of what she might have heard about their marital status. Unless the mistake had been made by James. Perhaps the assumption had been his?

She moved her shoulders in a dismissing shrug. She would have to deal with the problem later. Right now she would have to hurry to make herself and Rowan respectable.

Opening two of the cases, she looked through the clothes and selected finally the new navy blue all-in-one jump suit she had brought for Rowan. For herself she chose a woollen skirt checked in autumnal colours and a dark green V-necked sweater, the best wear, she knew only too well, for this climate and this house whose cool air was already beginning to seep into her bones. She changed her stockings, too, choosing some dark green, thick-textured ones, and thrust her feet into casual leather moccasins.

When she was dressed she brushed her hair standing in front of the big dressing table and tied a shiny white brown and green silk square with a jaunty knot about her neck. There, she looked much better, more in control, and there was actually a sparkle in her green eyes and a touch of natural colour in her normally pale cheeks as if as if ... oh, she might as well face it, as if she were looking forward to battling with Dermid again.

CHAPTER THREE

DINNER was served as it had always been served in the big draughty dining room. When Ellen entered the room with Rowan, Dermid was already sitting at one end of the long oval table, the glossy surface of which glowed with a deep reddish hue like his hair did now that it was brushed smoothly again. He had tightened his tie and had fastened his waistcoat again too, she noticed, before she turned to his aunt, Agnes Craig, who was sitting at the other end of the table.

With her narrow, slightly misshapen face and her hunched right shoulder which had been damaged at birth, Agnes Craig had always looked forbidding, and the dark plain clothes she wore didn't help to detract from that impression. She didn't move as Ellen approached her with Rowan but watched them coming to her with sorrowful dark brown eyes. When they stopped beside her she stared at Rowan for a few seconds, then suddenly her face crumpled.

'Oh, Ellen,' she whispered. 'You should have come before, you should have brought him before ... before Father died. He would have loved him.'

Sympathy awoke in Ellen and spread through her, softening the defensive, brittle attitude which had been building up within her ever since she had stepped off the plane. Bending forward, she put her arms around Agnes's thin wiry body and put her scented, firm cheek against the other woman's withered one.

'I'm sorry, Aunt Agnes, truly I am,' she murmured. 'I would have come before, only....' She broke off. Of what use were excuses now? She had let pride step in and prevent her from bringing Rowan to see his Scottish relatives in case Dermid had seen in such a move on her part an admittance of failure; failure to manage her life and her child without him. 'We're here now,' she said a little tremulously, withdrawing and smiling down at Agnes. 'And maybe our presence here will bring you some comfort. Rowan, this is your Aunty Agnes. Say hello to her and shake hands.'

'Where do you keep the dragon?' Rowan asked, gazing seriously at Agnes as he shook hands.

'In the cellar,' replied Agnes, rising to the occasion, and something bright twinkled in the depths of her eyes.

'Really?' said Rowan, his eyes widening with excitement. 'Can I see him?'

'Not now—you see, he's gone to sleep for the winter, like all the other animals that live underground,' said Agnes. She glanced down the table in Dermid's direction. 'He has a lisp just like you used to have, Dermid,' she added as Ellen led Rowan to a dining chair and helped him up on to it.

'That's what I thought,' drawled Dermid. 'And maybe for the same reason. Ellen, it could be that his tongue is tied. Mine was until the doctor attended to it. It's a small operation, best done when the child is young.'

'Did you used to suck your thumb too?' she asked him sweetly, taking her seat opposite Rowan.

'No, I expect he inherited that little trick from you,' he retorted, and the sardonic quirk of his mouth mocked her.

'You could get Ann to look at the lad's tongue tomorrow, if you like, when she comes to give me my injection,' said Agnes, completely unaware of any friction between her nephew and his wife.

'Ann?' queried Ellen, shaking out the starched linen table napkin and sliding it on to her knee as Bessie set down a bowl of soup in front of her. It was the old standby, Scotch broth, she noticed, thick with vegetables and swollen pearls of barley, and she couldn't help wondering if Bessie knew how to make any other sort of soup.

'Yes, Dr Ann Menteith. She's the daughter of a friend of mine,' said Agnes. 'She's the G.P. for this country area.'

'Ann was on the ferry,' put in Dermid. 'I had a few words with her at the pier. As usual she's worried about her children.'

'I expect she'd been over to see them. Her daughter and her son are both in boarding schools,' she explained to Ellen. 'She's a widow. Her husband was a research chemist and was killed when an experiment he was conducting blew up.'

'Don't want soup,' growled Rowan. 'Want peanut butter and jelly sandwiches.'

'Eat it,' ordered Dermid curtly.

'Don't like it,' said Rowan, and looking across the arrangement of small tawny and yellow chrysanthemums which was in the centre of the table Ellen saw that although he was scowling blackly his chin was wobbling ominously.

'How do you know you don't like it?' asked Dermid practically. 'You haven't tried it yet.'

'Not going to eat it,' muttered Rowan.

'Okay, please yourself, but I thought you said on the way here you were hungry,' argued Dermid.

'Dermid....' began Ellen, and he gave her a cold look.

'Shut up!' he said quite sharply, and she felt shock

ripple through that he had spoken to her so rudely in front of Agnes and the child.

'No, I won't,' she blurted. 'He's only a little boy....'

'If you'd only keep quiet and stop fussing over him he'll eat the soup and be glad to,' he retorted. 'Your conscience seems to be over-active where he's concerned. What are you trying to do? Make up for the hours you don't spend with him by being over-attentive to him when you are, by giving in to every little whim of his.'

'Dermid's quite right, you know,' said Agnes placidly. 'It doesn't do any good to fuss children. Ellen, when did you get your hair cut?'

Ellen's hand went involuntarily to the short fluffy bangs which curved above her forehead. Five years ago her hair had been very long, down past her shoulders, almost to her waist. She had worn it parted in the middle and held back from her face on either side by two tortoiseshell combs. Once when they had been making love Dermid had asked her never to have it cut.

'About two and a half years ago,' she said lightly.

'*Mummeee*, didn't you hear me? I want....' Rowan's voice came out in a low roar, but even so Dermid's voice, deep and authoritative, drowned out the rest of what the boy was saying.

'I suppose the short style is in keeping with the liberated female interviewer image,' he drawled. 'By the way, how's the job going lately?'

'Oh, all right, thank you,' she replied as Bessie came in with a tray and began to collect up the empty soup bowls. The housekeeper's hand was just reaching for Rowan's still full bowl when Dermid spoke brusquely again.

'Leave it, Bessie, and don't bring anything else for him just yet,' he said, and Ellen's nerves tingled with the natural urge to protect her child as if from an enemy.

'Very well, sir.' Bessie's face was wooden, expressing nothing of what she was feeling as she turned away to go and fetch the next course.

'Only all right, hmm?' said Dermid, leaning back in his high-backed chair, and his eyes held a wicked taunting gleam as they met Ellen's.

'Like any other job it has its ups and downs,' she replied stiffly. She must try to hang on to her cool, she thought, clenching her hands on her knees. She mustn't let him get under her skin with his mockery.

'Really?' he drawled. How infuriating was that upward tilt of his eyebrow, how aggravating the sardonic curve of his mouth! Once she had been fascinated by the way his upper lip curved back from his teeth when he smiled. She had loved to trace the curve with her forefinger. *God*, what was she going to do? She wanted to go and do that now, wanted to press her mouth against his, to stroke away the mockery with the soft movements of her lips, to tempt him into kissing her her instead of taunting her.

'I'd have thought it would be one long up,' he went on, 'a heady trip for your female ego, meeting all those exciting people—interviewing local politicians and celebrities, pop stars and super intellectuals, sharing the limelight with them.'

'Is that what you do, Ellen? I've often wondered.' Ellen's soft innocent voice floated down the length of the table. 'I should think you look very pretty on the television, dear,' the voice continued soothingly as Bessie came into the room again to set plates of roast beef before them. 'Dark-haired people always come across much better on the screen than fair people do, I always think,' Agnes chattered on. 'I like to watch those interview programmes. I wish your programme was shown here, then I could watch it and tell everyone else in the district to watch it. I suppose there isn't any chance of it ever being shown here?'

'No, I'm afraid not. It goes out only on a Canadian provincial network,' Ellen replied gently.

'But you must enjoy the work to want to keep on doing it,' persisted Agnes. 'And as Dermid says, it must be exciting meeting and talking with celebrities.'

'Not all the people I interview are celebrities. Some of them are ordinary persons who are doing an ordinary job of working but at the same time making a contribution to the community in which they are living with what they do in their leisure hours,' replied Ellen. 'They're not all politicians, or pop stars or intellectuals,' she added, sending a vindictive glance in Dermid's direction.

'It's so important for a woman to have an interest outside the home which has nothing to do with her children or her husband,' Agnes rattled on heedlessly. 'Don't you think so, Dermid?'

'Oh, every time,' he drawled. 'Spending time trying to winkle information out of someone who doesn't want to give it in front of T.V. cameras must be much more *satisfying* and *fulfilling* than staying at home all day looking after one small boy or being there when your husband comes home.'

Agnes missed the sarcastic inflection, but Ellen didn't. She glared at him and when he merely grinned at her she was very tempted to pick up her glass of water and throw the liquid in his face.

'This roast beef is really good, Aunt Agnes,' she said instead, determined to direct the conversation away from herself.

'I'm glad you like it, dear. Maybe the wee laddie will

have some when he's finished his soup. He seems to be managing to feed himself very well for one so young.'

Ellen looked quickly across the table. To her amazement Rowan was eating his soup slowly and with some difficulty because the silver spoon was too big for his mouth. Yet most of the soup was going in. Only a little of it dribbled down his chin on to the table napkin which was tucked into the collar of his jumpsuit.

She felt suddenly deserted, as if he had gone over to the enemy. He was doing exactly what Dermid had said he would do, yet for months both she and her mother had been trying, using both promises and threats, to persuade Rowan to eat the same food that they ate and they hadn't succeeded. And now after only a very short time with his father he was obeying the cool calm authority which Dermid knew only too well how to exert.

The spoon clattered in the empty bowl as Rowan put it down. He glowered at Ellen.

'Want some more,' he demanded.

'You can have some meat and vegetables now,' said Dermid before Ellen could speak.

'No! Want more soup.' Rowan transferred his aggressive stare to his father.

'Sorry, it's meat and vegetables or nothing. Think about it and let me know,' said Dermid coolly.

'He doesn't understand,' said Ellen, rushing in protectively.

'Oh yes, he does. He understands very well. He has quite a high intelligence quotient, I'd guess. That's why he had to get his own way with you. He got you just where he wants you.' Dermid's glance drifted over her in a slow sensually suggestive way. 'I wish I had,' he added softly, and again she felt the nerves in the lower part of her body flutter unexpectedly and the heat of desire scorch through her, and for a few moments she was oblivious to everything and everyone else in the room, her eyes held captive by the subtle invitation gleaming in the tawny-flecked darkness of Dermid's eyes.

Agnes spoke again and Ellen jumped, turning quickly to the other woman, wondering how much she had noticed. Her hand knocked the handle of her fork and it fell to the floor. With a muttered apology she bent down to retrieve it, glad of the opportunity to hide the hot colour which was flushing her cheeks.

It was ridiculous to feel this way just because a man had made a pass at her. For that was what Dermid had done. He wished he had her where he wanted her and she had no doubts about what he meant. He wanted her in bed, giving in to him, submitting to his physical desires.

She must keep reminding herself that physical attraction meant nothing to him. It didn't mean he loved her. She must remember that if she hadn't given in not only to his desires but to her own desires five years ago she wouldn't have married him.

Agnes was speaking again, telling her about the funeral of Neil Craig, about all the people who had attended it. While she listened Ellen watched Rowan eating up the mashed potatoes, chopped up meat, carrots and gravy which Bessie had brought for him. He was eating with an obvious enjoyment which irritated her because he had always refused such food before.

For dessert there was marmalade sponge pudding and creamy custard. Ellen could manage only a third of the helping in her dish, but Rowan ate every crumb of his and then scraped the custard which clung to the sides of the dish as if he feared it was the last food he would be offered for a while.

When he had finished he wiped his mouth not on the

napkin but on the back of his hand, pulled the napkin off and tossed it on to the floor and slid from the chair. Without hesitation he went to Dermid.

'Can I go out to play, now?' he asked.

'Where?'

'In the yard.'

'The garden, you mean,' said Dermid. 'Yes, of course you can.'

Ellen decided it was time she asserted herself. The garden was extensive. Rowan could easily wander from it into the pine forest and not find his way back again. Or he could be tempted to go down to the shore. Her imagination leaping ahead, she had him lost or drowned already.

'Rowan, I don't think you should go out just now,' she said. 'Wait until Mummy can come with you.'

'Why can't you come now?' he countered.

'Yes, Ellen, why don't you go now?' said Agnes, rising to her feet. 'It'll do you good to get out into the fresh air.'

'But I thought....' Ellen looked round at Dermid. He was pushing his chair back from the table. 'Won't the lawyer be coming this afternoon to read the will?' she asked, and about to rise to his feet, he flopped back in his chair and stared at her in surprise.

'Where did you get that idea?' he asked, his mouth curving mockingly. 'Have you forgotten it's Sunday and nothing ever happens on a Sunday here?'

'When is he coming, then? I haven't much time, only a week,' she said.

'I'd have thought you'd be entitled to more holiday than that,' he said sharply, his eyes narrowing.

'I've had my holidays for this year.'

'Have you? Then why didn't you bring Rowan over to see me?' he challenged.

'I ... er ...' She had thought of coming, had actually longed to come, but had been afraid to come in case she had found some other woman with him in the house at Kilruddock. 'You didn't invite me,' she muttered, rising to her feet.

'Ellen.' Dermid had also risen and was coming round the table towards her. She moved quickly in the other direction, skirting round Agnes's vacant chair, passing behind the one Rowan had sat on and made for the door through which Rowan and Agnes had already gone. But she didn't reach the door because Dermid had gone back round the other way and was there, stepping in front of her. 'I've often asked you to bring him here,' he said, frowning down at her.

'Bring *him*, yes,' she retorted. 'But never once have you invited *me* specifically to come. Never once have you invited *me*...!' Her voice broke and she pushed past him to leave the room. There was no sign of Rowan and Agnes in the hall, but Bessie was coming from the kitchen, tray in her hand, on her way to clear the dining room table.

'The laddie is away with Miss Agnes, to see where the dragon lives,' she said, a twinkle in her eyes.

'Thank you. I'm going to take him for a walk. I'm just going up to get a coat for him and a jacket for myself,' replied Ellen.

'Aye, ye'll need to dress warmly. For all the sun's shining now the wind's sharp,' said Bessie.

Up in the bedroom Ellen took time to unpack some of her clothing and hang it in the wardrobe. She carried Rowan's case into the dressing room and arranged his clothing in the chest of drawers. She worked quickly and methodically, concentrating on what she was doing, keeping her thoughts away from the most recent confrontation with Dermid. When the clothes were all unpacked she closed the three cases and put them neatly beside the wardrobe. Then she selected a green and white ski jacket which she had brought for just such an occasion as a walk along the shore or in the woods, put it on and zipped it up. Rowan could wear his quilted nylon hooded parka, it should be warm enough.

About to leave the room, she decided to take a head-square with her to tie over her hair to keep it from blowing about and was just closing the drawer in the dressing table from which she had taken it when the bedroom door opened. In the mirror she watched Dermid enter. His tie in his hand, his shirt collar was undone and he was flicking undone the buttons of his waistcoat.

He looked up, paused when he saw her, then kicked the door shut and leaned against it. The silence in the room as they stared at each other's reflections was so intense and complete that Ellen could hear the booming of the sea in the hollow rocks at the end of the headland the sound blown to her by the wind which lifted the lace curtains at one of the partially opened windows.

'Ellen, there's something I have to say to you,' Dermid began slowly, advancing into the room and pulling off his suit jacket.

'There's something I have to say to you, too,' she replied quickly, swinging round to face him, taking the initiative while she had the chance. 'I'm not sharing this room with you while I stay here. I'm not sleeping in that bed with you.'

His eyebrows went up, his eyes widened and for once he looked bewildered. He tossed his jacket down on the cretonne-covered armchair and as he slipped off his waistcoat he looked at the bed.

'The room is as good as any other in this house,' he

drawled, turning to sling his waistcoat down on top of the jacket. 'And the bed looks big enough.' One hand at his shirt front, slipping undone buttons, he slanted a derisive glance at her. 'There'll be plenty of room. It'll be like sleeping in twin beds, you on one side while I'm on the other. Not like having the ocean between us, but near enough. Of course if you'd feel safer we could always put some pillows down the middle....'

'Dermid, stop it!' Her voice was low and shaken.

'Stop what?'

'Taunting me, making fun, whatever you want to call it. This situation isn't funny and I'm being serious. I can't sleep in that bed with you.'

'Then where will you sleep?' he asked, only casually interested now, as he pulled the shirt tails out of the waistband of his trousers and slid his arms out of its sleeves. Bare to the waist, he turned away again to drop the shirt on his other clothes and in spite of her resolve not to look at him Ellen's glance swerved in his direction and clung, admiring the shift of muscles under skin which was still lightly tanned from exposure to the sun in the summer.

'You'll have to ask Bessie to make a bed up for you in another room,' she said, and to her intense irritation her voice lacked conviction.

'Oh no.' Still his back to her, he began to unbuckle the belt at his waist and still she didn't look away. 'It's you who doesn't want to sleep in here, so you can ask Bessie to make up a bed for you in another room,' he said coldly.

'But I have to stay and sleep near Rowan,' she argued weakly, her eyes following his movements shamelessly as he dropped his pants and stepped out of them. Blurred with dark hairs, his thighs were taut and muscular and she was still staring at them, as she was swamped suddenly by memories of the tenderly passionate physical intimacy they had once enjoyed and shared together when he swung round to face her, dressed only in his bikini-styled underbriefs which clung closely to him, disguising nothing.

'Well, well.' His voice was softly scoffing. 'Had a good look? Satisfied? Do I pass muster? Or would you like me to strip completely?' His thumbs hooked suggestively in the elasticised top of the briefs as if he were about to pull them down. 'On second thoughts perhaps you'd like to do that for yourself,' he continued mockingly. 'In bed, of course.' He stepped towards her and the sensuous expression in his eyes mesmerised her, rooting her to the spot where she stood. 'We have time, you know,' he said persuasively. 'All the rest of the afternoon, in fact, because Rowan is being quite adequately entertained by two other women. He doesn't need you. But I do.' He took another step forward so that the heady male smell of him was all about her and her senses reeled.

Still clutching Rowan's parka in front of her as if it were some sort of shield which would protect her from attack, her lips parting as she gasped for breath, her tongue licking her dry lips, her breasts tautening and lifting as they anticipated and longed for the touch of his finger-tips, Ellen stepped slowly backwards, unable to look away from him, and he came on, after her, the bare skin of his broad shoulders gleaming faintly gold in the afternoon sunlight which slanted in through the windows, the hairs which arrowed his wide chest glinting as darkly red as the wave of hair which slipped forward across his brow.

'Dermid, if ... if you dare to make me do it, it'll be rape,' she warned him, and had difficulty in shaping the word because her lips were so dry and tremulous.

'Will it?' The satirical tilt of one dark eyebrow mocked her. 'I doubt it, Ellen, I doubt it very much,' he drawled, moving towards her again, his bare feet quiet on the thick carpet. 'We're still married and....'

'But that doesn't give you the right to force yourself on me if I don't want you,' she protested desperately, afraid of her own responses if he touched her.

'Been interviewing some militant members of the feminist movement lately?' he queried mockingly. 'You seem to have their propaganda right on the tip of your tongue.'

'It isn't propaganda, it's the truth,' she retorted. 'I don't want you....'

'That isn't the impression I received when I turned round and found you staring at me, just now,' he scoffed softly, stepping right up to her and twitching the parka out of her clutching arms he tossed it away, not caring where it fell, not moving his gaze from his eyes. 'Come on, Ellen, relax a little. It's only natural for us to want to be together after all the time we've been apart, and maybe it'll relieve the tension, put everything back in its right perspective.'

'No, I can't, I won't. Oh, you must be very arrogant if you believe I want to make love with you knowing what I do about you,' she stormed. 'And if you dare to touch me I'll scream the place down!'

'No, you won't.' He was laughing at her, actually laughing at her.

'And even if you do no one will hear you,' he went on. 'The walls are thick in these old stone houses.' He stepped and his hands went to her waist. 'But you won't scream, Ellen, because you'll be enjoying yourself too much,' he added softly.

'I won't! And nothing you can do will make me

respond to you,' she asserted, trying to ignore the pressure of his hands.

'Nothing, Ellen?' The mockery in his eyes was a live and wicked thing, a dancing of golden light in the dark, coming nearer and nearer, hypnotising her into immobility. 'Not even this?' he queried.

'No, Derm....' Her denial came out not in a scream but in a weak whisper which was cut off short when his lips, cool and slightly parted, touched hers in a feather-light kiss. It was hardly the brutal bruising of her lips which she had expected, her mind full of the stories she had heard and read about men forcing their wives to submit to them, and she had a struggle to control the quivering response of her own lips to the tenderly coaxing movements of his.

She put her hands against his chest to push him away, but on touching the familiar hair-crisped skin they betrayed her too, moving of their own volition, fingers stroking and kneading, sliding up over the smooth bulk of his shoulders and expressing their pleasure in feeling him again, seeking and probing for potent nerve endings which were hidden in the hollows of his spine.

'Oh, Ellen!' He spoke in a sighing whisper against her mouth and at once her lips parted to welcome his. Somehow her jacket was open and his hand was sliding up under her sweater, fingers closing possessively over her breast, drifting and flicking tantalisingly against the silk-sheathed nipple. At once it seemed as if a flame scorched through her melting the tension which had held her nerves taut. Mind and body fused and, succumbing to the delicious sensuousness which was slowly consuming her, she leaned against him with a sigh of pleasure.

Standing in the middle of the room they clung in a close embrace, too absorbed in the delight of rediscovering each other's physical needs to hear the rattle of the doorknob as it was turned and the soft *shusshing* noise of a heavy door being pushed open.

'Mummy, I wanna go out and play, *now*!' Rowan's voice was shrill and insistent. 'Mummee ... what's that man doing to you?'

Dermid's crisp expressive oath was for her ears only, as was his muttered, 'I should have locked the bloody door!' Letting go of her, he swung round to answer his son just as Agnes who was hovering in the doorway answered Rowan's question.

'That man is your daddy, and I expect he's showing your mummy how much he loves her,' said Agnes, surprising Ellen by her calm acceptance of the situation, apparently not finding it the least strange to see her nephew dressed only in his underwear.

'Hasn't anyone ever told you that it's rude to barge into a bedroom without knocking on the door first?' Dermid's voice was harsh as he glared down at Rowan.

'Are you going swimming?' asked Rowan innocently, turning wrath away with a soft answer, and Ellen couldn't help her mouth twitching into a smile as thrusting his hand through his hair Dermid gave her an exasperated yet humorous glance. 'Is that why you have your swimsuit on?'

'Don't be angry with him, Dermid,' Agnes pleaded. 'I'm afraid he reached the door before I did. He can run up the stairs, I can't.' She placed a thin hand on her flat chest which was heaving slightly. 'I came to tell you....' She broke off and wheezed for breath, then continued, 'I came to tell you Mr Anderson the boat-builder from Portcullin is on the phone wanting to speak to you.'

'Thank you. I'll be down to speak to him as soon as I've put some clothes on,' replied Dermid, turning to unstrap his suitcase. 'You should have sent Bessie up with the message,' he went on, his voice suddenly gruff with concern. 'There's no need for you to be going up and down the stairs. Aren't you going to have your afternoon rest?'

'I think I will,' sighed Agnes. 'I was so enjoying myself with the wee laddie I forgot about resting.' Her glance went to Ellen and she smiled hesitantly. 'You won't mind, will you, Ellen?'

'No, no, of course not, Aunt Agnes. You have your rest and I'll see you later. At tea-time?'

'Yes, at tea-time.' Agnes smiled, looking comforted. 'We'll have it in the study before the fire. My father always liked to have it there on a Sunday afternoon.'

She drifted away from the doorway along the landing and Ellen picked up Rowan's parka from the floor.

'What's wrong with Aunt Agnes?' she asked as she bent before Rowan to help him put the parka on.

'She has a diseased valve in her heart,' replied Dermid, stepping into dark brown corduroys which were so sleek and smooth they looked like velvet. 'A result of having a severe dose of rheumatic fever as a child, so I've been told. Ann has suggested surgery, but it would be a fifty-fifty chance.'

Ann. How his easy casual use of that name irked her! How it brought to mind the woman at the ferry terminal. Ann, fair, fat and fortyish and looking for a man. Now, now, Ellen, don't be catty. Being catty about another woman just because your husband refers to her with easy familiarity suggests you're jealous of his association with that woman, and if you're jealous it means you're....

'Mummy, I love you too,' murmured Rowan, and wound his arms about her neck so that she couldn't stand up. She felt his lips warm and sticky from something he had eaten, possibly a sweet which Agnes had given him, pressing against her cheek.

'And I love you,' she whispered, returning the kiss, but he wasn't much interested. Out of the corners of his eyes he was watching Dermid put on a fine woollen shirt checked in browns and greens, obviously interested in his father's reaction to the conversation.

'Do you love him?' he asked, pointing a finger at Dermid who was now pulling on a soft green V-necked Shetland sweater. The more casual clothes made him seem more familiar to her. Once again he was the country-loving, sea-loving adventurer she had fallen in love with just over five years ago, the young and ardent husband who had brought her to this house to meet his grandfather because he had wanted her to see, to know and perhaps even love as much as he did, the place where he had grown up. 'Mummy,' Rowan's breath was hot on her mouth, 'do you love him as much as you love me?'

I did love him once. The answer formed in her mind as zipping up Rowan's parka she searched her mind for some other answer to distract the child without giving her away to Dermid—*Oh, you've no idea how much I loved him.*

'Now that, my lad, is a leading question.' Dermid's voice was mocking, slicing through her thoughts, and across the room his eyes challenged hers as he made for the door. 'And your mother is too much of a liberated woman to answer it honestly.'

'Well,' Ellen straightened up and zipping up her ski jacket again thrust her hands in its slanting pockets, 'you've got a nerve, Dermid Craig, butting in on a conversation and answering a question which was addressed to me,' she retorted, tilting her chin at him.

'And taking the words right out of your mouth?' he

put in wickedly, swinging the door open wider so he could go through it. 'But you can't answer his question honestly, can you? Because to answer it would be to commit yourself one way or the other. And commitment to another person, particularly a male person, is a sin in your eyes, isn't it? Now you've been brainwashed into believing love of a woman for a man or the other way round is nothing but an adolescent fantasy out of which it's necessary to grow if you're going to become a whole, truly integrated, fully independent person.'

'You....' she began.

'Now, now, Ellen, watch your language—think of the child,' he chided her, and was gone through the door, his laughter floating back to her from the landing, mocking the impotent fury which was suddenly smoking through her.

'Mummy ... *Mummee*!' Rowan was tugging at her skirt. 'You didn't tell me. Do you love that man as much as you love me?'

'No, I don't. I certainly do not,' Ellen said through her teeth.

'Let's go out—come on. I wanna play in the yard.'

Taking a deep breath in an effort to control the frustrated anger which was making her shake, Ellen let herself be pulled out of the room along the landing and down the stairs. On the way to the front door she and Rowan were just passing the doorway of the study when Dermid came out.

'I'm going to drive into Portcullin in the Rolls,' he announced, his glance slanted down at Rowan. 'How would you like to come with me, Rowan, to see some boats—some sailing boats?' he added softly, at his most persuasive. 'There's something I'd like to show you.'

'Mummy.' In his uncertainty the child turned automatically to her for guidance which was something she should be glad about, thought Ellen. But she could tell he was tempted to go with the attractive new person who in the space of a few hours had become a magnetic force in his life, pulling him away from her and from all he had known until today.

'We're going for a walk along the seashore to look for shells,' she said firmly, grasping Rowan's hand and turning towards the front door.

'You could come too, if you like,' said Dermid, but he didn't sound very encouraging. He wasn't wasting any of his powers of persuasion on her, she noticed with a touch of bitterness. He had stopped doing that three years ago. Unless she counted what had happened a short while ago in the bedroom upstairs. Heat flooded through her suddenly as she recalled what had happened or had nearly happened. She had nearly given in to him. If Rowan hadn't burst into the room, if someone hadn't phoned wanting to speak to Dermid by now they would have.... Oh, it didn't bear tthinking about.

'No, thank you,' she replied coolly, suppressing the urge she had to go with him to Portcullin. What was the point of going with him? They would only bicker all the time, and that wasn't good for the child. 'And I think Rowan should stay with me. He's still feeling strange here. Everything is so new to him he's quite bewildered.'

'Meaning I'm strange and new to him, I suppose.' Dermid's voice was dry and his mouth turned down at one corner. 'And I'm likely to go on being a stranger to him if you're going to keep him to yourself all the time, smother him with your possessiveness.'

'I'm not possessive!' she flared at him.

'No?' he jeered. 'Then prove it by letting him come with me this afternoon. You stay here, put your feet up, have a rest. You look as if you need one.' His glance raked her from head to toe and again his mouth quirked ironically at one corner. 'You look worn out,' he went on relentlessly. 'You have bags under your eyes which shouldn't be there and you're too thin. What have you been doing, Ellen, living on your nerves?'

'This sudden concern!' She took refuge in sarcasm because she didn't want him to know how sharply his comments on her appearance hurt her. 'What's it to you how I look or how I've been living?'

'You're my wife, Ellen,' he began, stepping towards her, his voice changing, softening.

'So you keep on saying,' she retorted. 'And that gives you rights, I suppose. The right to say and do what you like to me, the right to to ... take Rowan from me!' Her voice shook suddenly, uncontrollably, and she turned again to head for the door. 'Well, you're not going to! I'm not tired and I'm taking him for a walk. Go and look at boats by yourself!'

She strode towards the front door, pulling Rowan after her, aware that he was beginning to whine. The old-fashioned brass door-knob turned under her hand and the door opened more easily than she had expected. At once the wind swept in, wrenching the door from her hand and slamming it back on its hinges. The rugs rippled and lifted on the shiny floor and in the rear of the house open doors banged shut. The whole place was full suddenly of noise and movements and through the open door of the study came the tangy whiff of woodsmoke, blown from the fire.

'Shut the door!' yelled Dermid, and striding across took hold of the door and swung it hard into the teeth of the wind, pushing it closed with the weight of his shoulder behind it. At once the house became quiet again. 'We never open it when the wind is in the west,' he rasped angrily. 'Don't you remember from the last time you stayed here?'

'No, I don't. I wasn't here for very long and it was five years ago. How could I remember?' she countered, swinging round to face him.

'That's right, rub it in,' he grated through taut lips and, glaring at her with nearly black eyes. 'I'm getting the message, loud and clear. What you're really saying is that you don't want to remember anything you've done with me and you don't want to do anything or go anywhere with me, now. Right?'

'No. I ... er ... I don't know. Oh, you've got me all confused!' she complained.

'Have I? Now that's interesting,' he jeered. 'Then of course you would like to be relieved of my company, be on your own. Go on, then, go for your walk. I'll hold the door for you and close it afterwards—but remember when you come back, use the side door.'

'Dermid, I ... I'm. ...'

'If you say you're sorry I'll wring your neck,' he grated in a savage undertone, and opened the door cautiously, wide enough for her to slide out and pull Rowan after her. As soon as they were out the door was closed quietly after them.

'Aren't we going to see the boats?' Rowan's voice trembled querulously as they went down the steps, pushing into the wind which stung their faces and snatched their breaths away.

'Not today, darling,' muttered Ellen. 'A walk will do us good,' she added in a louder, more determined voice in an effort to convince herself as much as the child. In spite of the brightness of the sunshine the weather was really too cold to go walking at the snail's pace which Rowan walked. It was an afternoon for brisk movement.

'Don't wanna go for a walk,' Rowan wailed miserably. 'Wanna go to see boats!'

Gritting her teeth, Ellen dragged him after her along the narrow gravel path edged by flower borders in which dwarf chrysanthemums and the odd pink rose were still blooming. When she reached the single gate between two stone pillars she swung it open and stepped through on to the lane which separated the garden from the shore. Grizzling and sobbing and trying to wrench his hand free of hers, Rowan went with her across the lane to follow another well-worn path which twisted down among lichen-patched rocks to the firm damp brown sand where long ropes of olive-brown seaweed, wet and rubbery, lay entwined, left there by the high tide. Beyond the stretch of sand the water of the sea loch glinted and heaved, the colour of chilled sapphire and the distant islands were purple-black shapes against a pale azure sky tinted with the apricot glow of a sun which was slowly sliding down towards the horizon.

'Don't wanna be here. Wanna go with that man!' moaned Rowan. Tears poured from his eyes and ran down his cheeks which were tinged bluish-red by the cold sea-wind. Tugging his hand free of hers at last, he sat down abruptly on the wet seaweed and howled bitterly, his clenched fists knuckling his eyes.

Oh God, what was she going to do now? With one hand clenched in the pocket of her ski jacket Ellen rubbed the other across her own eyes as she felt them prick with tears of frustration and disappointment too. How tired she felt! Too tired to cope any more. Then why didn't she agree to Dermid's suggestion? Why didn't she stay in the house, put up her feet and rest while he took Rowan with him? Why didn't she let David find out at first hand what his son was like when he was in a contrary, stubborn mood? By insisting on keeping the child with her it looked as if she was only ruining her own relationship with Rowan.

Quickly, on sudden impulse, she bent down and grasping Rowan's hand pulled him to his feet.

'Come on, then,' she urged him. 'You can go with him to see the boats this afternoon. But hurry, he'll be leaving in a minute.'

Sniffing and hiccuping, Rowan went willingly with her, his little legs running, his feet hardly touching the ground as she hurried across the sand. Back across the lane they went, through the gate and up the garden path, round the corner of the house into the courtyard just in time to see the rear of the Rolls as it turned through the big double gateway on to the road. The soft purr of its engine as it took the hill came back to them like mocking laughter.

Rowan let out an anguished wail of disappointment and Ellen cringed inwardly. Squatting before him while blown bronze leaves rustled about the courtyard, she took him in her arms.

'Don't cry, honey, please,' she whispered. 'It's my fault—I should have let you go in the first place. But I'm so afraid of him, so afraid he'll take you from me.' Realising he couldn't possibly understand what she was talking about, she broke off and rubbed her cheek against his wind-chilled wet one and her tears mingled with his.

How bewildered he must be feeling, as bewildered as she was, not yet adjusted to the change of place and climate; above all not yet adjusted to the strong-willed, self-confident, quick-witted man who was his father and her husband.

'Go to see boats tomorrow,' said Rowan uncertainly, pulling away from her, staring at her with troubled eyes as if he sensed she was distressed as much as he was. 'Go for a walk now ... in the woods.'

'Not by the sea?' she asked, wiping the wetness from her cheeks on the back of her hand and smiling a little because after all he had the resilience to bounce back after being deeply disappointed.

'No.'

This time it was he who took her hand, leading her across the garden at the back of the house along a path, thick with leaves which crunched under their footsteps, through the shrubbery of dark-leaved rhododendron bushes and shiny-leaved holly into the green gloom of the resin-scented pine woods where the wind sighed in the branches and the water in a nearby stream tinkled merrily as it slipped over rocks.

CHAPTER FOUR

EVEN on a cold wind-torn day in late autumn the woods had always been peaceful and five years ago she had often walked in them with Dermid, holding hands, pausing to kiss every so often, typical honeymooners. Ellen's mouth twisted in a grimace of pain and the cold air which she breathed in suddenly and sharply as she gasped was raw against the back of her throat. Dermid had been right, just now. She didn't want to remember anything she had done with him because to remember was to hurt deeply inside. It was to yearn achingly for those lost times when anything she had done with him had been a special delight when he had only to look at her, his warm brown glance caressing her, and she had followed where he had led, never questioning, never doubting that anything they did together would be a joyous experience.

And while she had followed where he had led they had been happy. It was only when she had wanted to go along a different path from him that tension had sprung them apart. Because he hadn't been able to accept the fact that she could act independently of him? No, that wasn't so. He had accepted the fact that she wanted to work, had said she must take the job she had been offered if doing it would make her feel happy. But he hadn't stayed around to find out if it had made her happy. He hadn't cared enough.

Along a path matted with pine needles she strolled with Rowan, occasionally pausing to stand at the edge of the stream and look down into the clear sparkling water to see if any trout lurked there, sometimes bending to collect pine cones with him which they stuffed in their pockets to take back to the house to burn on the fire at tea-time, and all the time her thoughts were busy sifting over the problem of her marriage to Dermid as she tried to face up to the reality of the situation.

It was he who had insisted on separation in the first place. When she had shown him that she wanted to be more than just his bedmate, more than Mrs Dermid Craig, his wife and mother of his son, he had removed himself and had stayed away. Why had he done that? Why had he never come to visit her in Ottawa? If he had come at the end of that first year of separation how glad she would have been to see him. If he had sunk his pride once, enough to ask her to give up her job and go back to live with him in Scotland, she would have gone without hesitation because she had learned by then that no job, however interesting and demanding, could take the place of her relationship with him. Without his presence in her life everything she had done was lacking in value.

But he hadn't come to Ottawa at the end of that first year for Christmas and New Year as she had hoped. Her mother's cousin Sheila Moffatt, who had once been Sheila Rose, had come instead. A widow in her early sixties, she had been travelling about the world since her husband's death visiting relatives and had been invited by Janet to spend the festive season in Ottawa.

Since Sheila's son Ian also worked for Craig & Rose as a technologist Ellen had assumed she would have some news of Dermid, but she had received no satisfaction from Sheila's rather vague dismissing remarks about him, although she had learned that Dermid had been in South America helping to commission a new spinning factory which had been built for a Colombian textile company and on his return to Scotland had been promoted to the position of assistant manager of the technology department at Craig & Rose. About his personal life or whether he had sent any verbal messages to her by way of Sheila she had learned nothing. She had only the Christmas greeting card he had sent her and the present he had sent for Rowan.

It was not until after Christmas and New Year celebrations were over that she had heard Sheila say anything else about Dermid, and then it had not been during a conversation with herself. Returning from work one day Ellen had, as usual, spent some time with Rowan and had put him to bed, and it had been when she was going to sit in the living room with her mother and Sheila that she had heard Dermid's name mentioned. At once she had hesitated in the hallway and had leaned against the wall beside the archway which led into the room out of sight of the two women sitting in the room but able to hear everything they said.

'I've never been able to get over the way Neil Craig, his grandfather, took him under his wing after Maxwell's death,' Sheila had said. 'Mind you, I believe Maxwell's last words to his father just before he died in hospital after that accident were, "take care of the lad—Kate Allen's lad—he's mine." Can you imagine how mortified Barbara was when she heard that?'

'Yes, I can,' Janet had agreed. 'Neil Craig adopted Dermid, didn't he, so that he could be legally responsible for him?'

'That's right, and you can be sure Dermid has kept in with his grandfather with an eye to the main chance. He's an ambitious devil, there's no doubt about that. Ian was bitterly disappointed when Dermid was appointed assistant manager over his head even though

Dermid is younger than he is. Of course I'm sure Neil Craig had a hand in that.'

'I wouldn't be at all surprised,' Janet had commented, 'although I daresay Dermid is good at his job and he hasn't cared how much he's neglected his wife and child because of his work.'

'Och, I'm not denying he's clever and that he works hard, but it seems all wrong to me that someone lacking in morals like him is appointed to a job of responsibility when someone like my Ian who has always been a good-living, God-fearing man is passed over.' There had been a slight pause and a rustle of movement as if Sheila had changed her position. Then her voice had come, pitched a little lower. 'I haven't said anything before because I didn't want to upset Ellen too much,' she had said in a loud whisper, 'but the way Dermid has been carrying on with one of the girls in the typing pool at the factory has been disgraceful. Everyone has been talking about it!'

'What do you mean by carrying on?' Janet had asked.

'Well ... er ... she lives in the same suburb of Kilruddock that he does and when he's at home he gives her a lift to the office every morning and takes her back every night.'

'But that doesn't mean he's having an affair with her,' Janet had protested. 'Ellen is often given a lift to and from the studios by Walter Stewart, her boss, but I'm pretty sure it means nothing.'

'Aye, but Ellen is different from the little bitch I'm talking about,' Sheila had said rather sharply as if she had resented Janet's suggestion that she was exaggerating. 'She makes no secret of the fact that there's something between them, has been talking and giggling about it in the women's toilets at the factory and has even admitted that she spent the night with him several times at the house in Kilruddock. But then what can you expect, Janet, when you consider what his father and his mother were like? I think Ellen was a fool to marry him.'

'She was very young at the time,' said Janet with a sigh. 'I don't think she knew what she was doing either.'

'It's a pity about the little boy,' Sheila had gone on. 'I always think it's the children who suffer most when the parents are separated.'

'Rowan can hardly suffer much. He doesn't know his father,' Janet had replied.

'Just as well he doesn't, I'd say....'

Ellen hadn't stayed to hear any more but had crept upstairs to her bedroom, racked by the raw pain which had been slicing through her as Sheila's words had resounded through her mind over and over again. *A girl in the typing pool.... She's admitted she's spent the night with him several times...!*

And after the initial sharp pain had come disillusion, cancer-like, eating into her love for Dermid. The girl in the typing pool was the reason why he hadn't come to Ottawa to see her. He had turned from her just as Maxwell Craig had turned from his wife and had found consolation with another woman. That was why he hadn't even written to her.

But a letter had come from him at last, arriving after Sheila Moffatt had left. It had been a cool straightforward note saying he was sorry he hadn't been in touch with her but with the new responsibilities at work he hadn't been able to find the time to fly over and see her and Rowan. He asked after her health and how the job was going, if she was enjoying it. He had asked after Rowan, saying how much he would like to see him. He had suggested that when she had a holiday she should fly to Scotland with the child and possibly leave him there for a while to live. He had mentioned that he had bought a small yacht and had enjoyed racing it on the Clyde and cruising in it amongst the islands during the summer months. There had been nothing lover-like in the letter and there had been no direct appeal to her to give up her job and go back to live with him again.

With the knowledge that it was possible he had been unfaithful to her during the year of separation still sharp in her mind Ellen had replied, also coolly straightforward. She had told him she was enjoying her job and had no intention of giving it up. She had said Rowan was well and happy and that it would be some time before she could fly to Scotland with him. She had made it quite clear to him that separation from him was suiting her very well, and many months had passed before she heard from him again.

Oh, why didn't either of them admit it was over, their love affair and their marriage? Why try to cling to the tattered remnants of a dream? Why not admit that they had married for wrong reasons, that their relationship had been based purely on physical desire which had fizzled out after less than two years of marriage?

But had it fizzled out? God, no, it hadn't! Ellen's hands clenched in her pockets and she gritted her teeth in an attempt to control the heat of desire which once more scorched through her body and left it trembling when she remembered what had happened so recently in the bedroom at Inchcullin House. Dermid still possessed the power to rouse her, to tune every nerve in her body to taut tingling awareness. In fact he was the only man she had ever known who could do that, for in the process of her work she had met other men, had allowed them to take her out, but not one of them, handsome and sensually attractive as some of them had been, had been able to turn her on just by looking at her as Dermid could.

'Mummee, *Mummee*!' Rowan was tugging at her skirt, shouting at her to get her attention. He shrieked suddenly and flung his arms about her thighs, and looking down she was surprised to see a golden Labrador dog sniffing around them, wagging its plume-like tail excitedly. Raising its head, it stepped closer and licked Rowan's face so that the child shrieked again, although whether in fear or delight Ellen couldn't be sure.

'Tiger, come to heel, damn you! Yon laddie doesn't want ye to wash his face.'

The voice was rough and masculine and had a strong Scottish accent, and the dog obeyed the authority in it, slinking back up the path, only to turn and pad back at the heels of the man who was coming down it. A couple of feet distant from Ellen and Rowan the man stopped. Of medium height, he had longish black hair which brushed the collar of the short denim jacket he was wearing over a woollen tartan shirt. Sturdy muscular legs moulded his denim jeans and there was an arrogant jauntiness about him as he stood there with a shotgun slanted across his shoulders.

'Why have you got a gun?' asked Rowan, pushing away from Ellen and staring up at the man.

'Ach, well now, I'm carrying it in the hopes of shooting a pheasant or two, this afternoon,' replied the man.

'Do you have permission to shoot in these woods?' demanded Elllen, thinking that possibly he was a poacher.

'I do, permission from the owner himself,' he replied

easily, and there was something familiar about his glinting black eyes and mischievously slanting mouth. 'You don't remember me, do you, Ellen?'

Another memory of the time she had spent in Inchcullin five years ago tumbled into her mind to join the memories of times shared with Dermid which were tormenting her. It was the memory of the visit to a farmhouse somewhere near. An old whitewashed mullion-windowed place it had been, situated amongst gently sloping hills and surrounded by golden harvest-shorn fields. Dermid had taken her there to meet his mother—Kate Mackinnon as she had become after her marriage to Hector Mackinnon, farmer, a year or so after Maxwell Craig's death—and also to meet his two half-sisters and his half-brother.

'You're Angus, aren't you?' she exclaimed. 'Angus Mackinnon. Why, you've grown up!' In her memory he had been a coltish, mischievous seventeen-year-old who had liked to torment her.

'And so have you,' he retorted, his bold black glance assessing her with a slow insolence. 'And for the better, I'm thinking,' he added insinuatingly. His glance flicked down to the bright head of the now silent, thumb-sucking Rowan. 'By God, Dermid would have a hell of a job denying that lad is his, wouldn't he? He's surely left his mark on him. What's his name?'

'Rowan.'

'Ha!' his mocking laugh irritated her. 'That's a bit fancy, isn't it? But I can see why you've called him that.' He squatted before the boy in a quick lithe movement. 'Hello there, Rowan. Do you know who I am?'

Rowan shook his head from side to side and continued to suck his thumb while he stared at Angus with wary eyes.

'I'm your uncle.' Again Angus laughed. 'Och, I can hardly believe it myself. I'm your half-uncle. Your dad and I have the same mum. You can call me Angus. Can you say that?' Rowan nodded. 'And this is Tiger,' added Angus, holding the dog by the ruff of hairs round its neck as it rubbed itself against his bent knees. 'He won't bite you. He's just young like yourself and wants you to know he's friendly when he licks you. You give him a pat to show you're friendly too.'

Rowan obeyed and Angus straightened slowly to his full height, his long-lashed black eyes slanting a curious glance at Ellen's face which lingered there in frank sensual appraisal so that she felt irritation begin to simmer within her.

'So ye've come back,' he commented. 'Staying long?'

'What business is that of yours?' she retorted.

'None, I suppose, just that I'm a wee bit surprised to find ye walking in these woods this afternoon. The last I heard of ye ye were holding down some fancy T.V. job in Canada and had no time to come and visit your *relative* here in Scotland.'

The mocking emphasis he put on the word relative irritated her even more.

'Are you on your way over to see my mother?' he went on. 'Are you taking her first grandchild to see her?'

'No, I'm not.' She spoke shortly, then realising he might go back to Kate Mackinnon and tell her that her daughter-in-law was not disposed to visit her, she added quickly, 'At least not to-day. Rowan and I are just out for a walk. We're going back now to have tea with Aunt Agnes.' Taking Rowan's hand in hers she turned her back on Angus and began to go down the path.

'Then I'll walk along with you for a wee while,'

said Angus, falling into step beside her. 'Is Dermid at the house?'

'No, not right now. He's gone to Portcullin.'

'I expect he's gone to see Alec Anderson the boat-builder to find out what progress Alec is making with the building of his new yacht,' said Angus casually.

'Dermid is having a new yacht built?' exclaimed Ellen, without thinking.

'Didn't you know?' mocked Angus. 'Tut, tut, I'd have thought he'd have told you everything.'

'There hasn't been much time to talk about everything,' she retorted defensively. 'Rowan and I only arrived this morning. What sort of a yacht is it?'

'Ach, a big forty-foot ketch, expense no object now he's in the money. But you'll know all about that, won't you, Ellen—about the money, I mean? It didn't take you long to make your mind up about which side of the Atlantic you wanted to be when you heard *that* news,' Angus scoffed.

'What news? What are you getting at?' Ellen demanded, coming to a stop and swinging round on him. He stopped in his tracks too and turned to face her, his black eyes glinting with devilment.

'Ach, come on now, Ellen, don't pretend you don't know Dermid has inherited most of his grandfather's money,' he jeered. 'Isn't that why you've come running back to him, hoping for a share in the loot? But you'll have your work cut out if you want to hang on to him. You're not the only woman in Dermid's life, you know. You've got competition, and some of it is right here in Portcullin—and I wouldn't mind betting if that's where he goes after he's been to see Alec....'

'You've got a wicked mischievous tongue, Angus Mackinnin!' Ellen accused furiously. 'What are you trying to do? Make trouble between Dermid and me?'

'I don't have to, do I?' he retorted. 'There's trouble enough between you already. Dermid has never said anything, but we've all drawn our own conclusions. We know you and he live separately and go your own ways, so it won't come as a shock to anyone if he divorces you. I mean, what good is a wife if she doesn't keep a man's bed warm and have his supper ready for him when he comes in from work? I'll make damned sure mine does when I get married.'

'Oh, I should have guessed your mind would run in that groove,' she snapped at him. 'But you'll be lucky if any woman wants to marry you when she finds out you have those old-fashioned ideas. You're behind the times.'

'And I like it that way,' he replied with a grin. 'What's been good enough for my father will be good enough for me. I've never heard him complain about my mother or want to live apart from her. Nor have I ever heard her say she's bored with being a farmer's wife.' He broke off and stiffened, his eyes narrowing, his head tilting to one side as he listened. 'Be seeing you, Ellen,' he whispered, and moving silently and stealthily, the dog at his heels, he disappeared into the green gloom of the forest.

'Where's the man gone?' lisped Rowan.

'Hunting,' said Ellen shortly, turning and walking down the path again, and a few seconds the sound of a shot echoed through the woods.

All the way back to the house Angus's remarks rankled in her mind. How could he possibly know that Dermid had inherited his grandfather's money if the will hadn't been read yet? He must have been guessing, hoping perhaps that she would know something and tell him. She suspected there was a lot of local curiosity about what had been left to whom and who would benefit the most from the will of one of the wealthiest men in that part of the country.

But what rankled most was Angus's suggestion that Dermid was considering divorcing her. Was that the something he had wanted to talk about when he had walked into the bedroom earlier that afternoon? The subject which had also been on her mind and which she had brought up in the Rolls when he had accused her of being too hysterical to discuss anything? They hadn't discussed it in the bedroom because something else had happened, something she hadn't believed could happen between them any more.

And yet, and yet... Ellen felt suddenly chilled again as she recalled the bitter words they had flung at each other later in the hall. *I'm getting the message*, he had said. But what message? The message she had conveyed to him by her own behaviour? By the wild words spoken out of bewilderment and distrust? Was it possible he had taken them to mean she didn't want to have anything to do with him ever again?

'I'm tired, Mummy,' sighed Rowan. 'Carry me. Give me a piggyback.'

Obediently she bent down so he could lean against her back and put his arms about her neck. Putting her hands under his legs, she lifted them around her waist and stood up. Along the path she plodded, feeling his head resting heavily against hers. The woods were growing grey and shadowy as the sun slid closer to the horizon and through the trees she could see lights winking from the house.

Down into the shrubbery the path dropped and as she entered the courtyard she could see the water of the sea-loch glowing like molten bronze between purple-black headlands. The wind had died away and above the tracery of bare branches at the back of the house the round face of the moon peeped, the colour of bleached orange.

Ellen remembered suddenly it was Hallowe'en and wished she was a child again, going from house to house in the suburb of Ottawa where she had grown up, 'tricking and treating'. Perhaps next year Rowan would be old enough to go and she would accompany him. There was so much fun she and Rowan could have together, unless, unless.... Oh, no, she mustn't let that happen. She mustn't let Dermid divorce her and win custody of Rowan. She mustn't let him be so cruel to her.

It was surprisingly warm in the house and the fire in the study crackled merrily. Aunt Agnes was there to welcome with her vague sweet smile, and for a short time while she sat drinking hot weak tea and eating hot buttered scones with home-made strawberry jam Ellen was able to pretend that everything was all right, that there was no tug-of-war between her and Dermid, that soon he would come back from Portcullin to join them for tea and to tell them about his new yacht.

After the meal was over she took Rowan upstairs to bath him in the huge old-fashioned bathroom. When he was dressed in his pyjamas and was hugging his teddy bear she tried to persuade him to climb in the cot in the dressing room. But he would have nothing to do with it and insisted on sleeping in the big bed in the room allotted to her and Dermid. So she gave in and tucked him up in sheets and blankets which had been warmed by the electric blanket Bessie had thoughtfully provided. She sat with him for a few minutes telling him a story, but it wasn't long before his eyelids drooped and he fell fast asleep.

Not quite sure what to do with herself, she wondered when Dermid would return, trying to ignore the possibility which was nagging in her mind as a result of what Angus had said that he wouldn't return because he had gone to visit another woman in Portcullin; she decided to change her clothes. She might as well be looking her best if Dermid did come in and she had often found that dressing up in something exotic did something for the morale. She was glad she had decided to bring the long evening gown of dark red velvet, she thought, as she surveyed herself a few minutes later in the long wardrobe mirror. Its simple style, close-fitting low-cut bodice and softly flaring skirt flattered her slim waist and full bosom and the deep rich colour made her skin look whiter and her softly curling hair look even brighter.

'How pretty you look, dear,' said Agnes, who was after all the only person in the study when Ellen entered it again. 'Is the bairn asleep?'

'Yes, he's worn out.'

'And no wonder. It's a busy day he's had.'

'Is ... is Dermid back from Portcullin yet?' Ellen asked, sinking down into a leather-covered armchair on the opposite side of the fire from Agnes.

'No, he phoned while you were upstairs to say he wouldn't be back before ten and that you weren't to wait up for him if you're tired.'

'Did he say what had delayed him?' Ellen tried not to let her disappointment show in her voice, but even so it quivered a little.

'No, but then he never does. Quite a law unto himself is Dermid and always has been, and it doesn't do to question him about where he is or why he's going to be late,' said Agnes with a sigh. 'But you should know that by now, my dear. You've been married to him for—how long is it? Four years? I'm afraid my memory always was poor.'

'Five,' said Ellen tonelessly, staring into the heart of the fire. 'Aunt Agnes, have you any idea of what's in Grandfather Craig's will?'

'Of course I do, dear. Everyone does.'

'Everyone? But how can everyone know if it hasn't been read yet?'

'Not read yet?' Agnes looked puzzled and worried. 'But I'm sure....' she began, then broke off and started again in more confident tones. 'Yes, I'm quite sure it was read last Tuesday after the funeral. He left everything to Dermid, quite rightly so too, since he is his only heir, his shares in the company and this house and the land it stands on.'

'But what about you, Aunt Agnes, didn't he leave anything to you?'

'Yes, of course he did. I have an annuity which will keep me in comfortable style for some years and Dermid only has the house provided I'm allowed to continue to live in it. Oh, and he left numerous other bequests. My father was very generous. He didn't forget anyone, not even his great-grandchild, even though he had never seen him.' Agnes's brown eyes were sorrowful and reproachful as she looked across at Ellen. 'But that's why you've come, isn't it, to hear that part of the will. Father insisted that you and the child had to be here before that part was read.'

'Yes, but....' Ellen bit her lips hard. Angus hadn't been guessing after all. And there was no point now in telling Agnes that Dermid had told her nothing of what was in his grandfather's will. All she knew about it was the tersely-worded lawyer's letter requesting her presence in this house today when the will would be read. She hadn't realised that there was a separate part of the will concerning only Rowan.

But it hadn't been read today because it was Sunday. Then when would it be read? She would have to wait up until Dermid came in to ask him. She and he had to talk things out, not wrangle and backbite. They had to sit down calmly and coolly like the civilised people they were supposed to be and discuss their problems thoroughly for Rowan's sake. For Rowan's sake—the words repeated themselves over and over like the chorus of a song. She had been invited to come for Rowan's sake and she must keep that in front of her mind all the time she was with Dermid.

'It's nice having you here,' Agnes's soft voice broke in on her thoughts. 'Are you going to stay here long?'

'Only until I know what was in the will for Rowan,' replied Ellen. 'And then I think I'll go over to Ayr and stay with my mother's cousin Sheila Moffatt for a few days before flying back to Canada next Saturday.'

'Oh, I see.' Agnes expressed her disappointment. 'I hoped you'd stay longer than that.' She looked very worried for a few minutes, her lips twitching, her thin claw-like hands pulling nervously at the stuff of her dress on her knees. 'Ellen, I don't like to interfere in other people's lives ... but do you think it's wise to live so far away from Dermid?' she asked timidly. 'I know I've never been married.' She grinned suddenly and lifted her shoulders in a funny little shrug. 'I've never even had a boy-friend,' she confessed with an endearing giggle, 'so I have very little experience of such relationships, but my father always used to say he thought the way you and Dermid were living imposed an intolerable strain on both of you. He wasn't at all happy about it.'

'No, I don't suppose he was,' sighed Ellen, staring into the fire again.

'He was always a good-living man and was very

disappointed in the way my brother Maxwell behaved,' Agnes rushed on as if afraid to stop now that she had dared to speak what was on her mind. 'He did hope that when Dermid married you the boy would settle down and not....' Agne's mouth began to tremble and tears gathered in her brown eyes. 'Oh, Ellen,' she whispered, 'you've no idea how the stories about Dermid's association with other women hurt him. He was able to ignore the one your mother's cousin spread about Dermid's friendship with the girl at the office, but when gossip started up here about Dermid and Dr Menteith and then about Dermid and Ann's daughter Morag....'

'Daughter? The doctor has a daughter old enough...?'

'Morag is seventeen,' said Agnes. 'And she and Ann went sailing with Dermid this past summer cruising up to Skye and out as far as Stornoway and .... well, people talked.'

'Naturally, they always do,' said Ellen dryly. So Ann Menteith and her daughter were the competition Angus had referred to. Well, having seen the fair Ann she knew she had it in her to deal with that competition, but about the daughter she was not so sure. A man of Dermid's age might easily be turned on by a fresh young woman just out of boarding school....

'You think that's all it might be, then, talk?' asked Agnes hopefully. 'I do hope you're right, Ellen. Father said it might be, but he blamed you for it. He said that if you'd been living here in Scotland with Dermid people wouldn't have made such suggestions.'

'Did he ever tell Dermid how he felt about the gossip?'

'Yes, he did. It was the only time I've ever known Dermid to lose his temper with his grandfather. He was very angry and didn't come to see us for several weeks afterwards. Poor father, he was much distressed.'

'And what about Dr Menteith? How does she react to the gossip?' asked Ellen.

'I really don't know, dear, I've never mentioned it to her,' said Agnes at her most prim. 'You see, Ellen, it isn't done to talk about such things to one's doctor, and Ann is always very professional when she comes to see me. We talk only about my illness and the weather.'

'Where does she live?'

'In Portcullin. Ellen, my dear, you've gone very white.' Agnes leaned forward anxiously. 'I've upset you, haven't I. I shouldn't have mentioned the gossip. But if ... if Father had been alive he would have mentioned it to you. He was so concerned, you see, about Dermid, and....'

At that point there was a knock on the study door, it opened and Bessie looked in.

'I'm thinking it's time ye were on y'r way to bed, Miss Agnes,' she said. 'The doctor will be coming bright and early in the morning, to check up on ye, Mr Dermid said. And ye want to be at y'r best for her, don't ye?'

'All right, Bessie ... I'm coming.' Agnes pushed herself slowly up from her chair. 'You won't mind, Ellen, if I go up now? You look tired too, so don't sit here for long. Have a good night's rest and you'll be able to cope with everything much better tomorrow.'

After kissing Agnes goodnight Ellen sank back into her chair and stared at the red-hot heart of the fire, hearing the voices of the other two women fade to a murmur as they crossed the hall to the stairs.

It was nine o'clock. Another hour to wait for Dermid, and even then he might not come. What was he doing? It was easy to guess after what she had just learned about Ann Menteith. She sprang to her feet and paced about the room, the skirt of the long red dress flirting out every time she changed direction.

How had she got herself into this humiliating position? she wondered, striking one hand against the other and then holding them clenched together close to her breast. Here she was, alone and waiting for her errant husband to return home after visiting his mistress. It didn't happen to people like her. It happened to other women, but not to her. It happened to women like her mother's cousin Barbara, Maxwell's wife, but not to her. And she wasn't going to let it happen. She wasn't going to give Dermid the satisfaction of finding her waiting for him. She was going to bed to sleep even though it was early.

She had left one small lamp lit on the dressing table in the bedroom as a night light for Rowan. By its rosy glow she could see he was sleeping deeply, his cheeks flushed pink and hair gleaming bright against the pillow. She undressed quickly, put on her nightgown and dressing gown and went along the landing to the bathroom. When she came back she laid her dressing gown on a chair near the bed, turned off the light and climbed into the bed.

There was plenty of room, as Dermid had said, room enough for him as well as Rowan and herself, if he came. But he wouldn't be coming to sleep in here. His suitcase had gone and she guessed he had asked Bessie to make up another bed for him in another room. Unless ... the thought cut through her like a knife ... unless he had taken it to Portcullin with the intention of not returning tonight; with the intention of staying with Ann Menteith?

She groaned and twisted on to her stomach, the thought of him with Ann making it churn as if she was going to be sick. She mustn't think about it any more, she would go crazy if she did. She must calm down and go to sleep like a child, like Rowan, as if she hadn't a care in the world. She closed her eyes and mercifully, almost at once, the blanket of sleep enfolded her.

It was out of that thick dark blanket which had smothered her thoughts and had brought her temporary release that she struggled two hours later, aware of voices speaking nearby. One was deep and masculine, speaking softly yet with firm authority. The other was a child's treble. So deeply had she been sleeping that her eyelids seemed to be glued together and she had difficulty in unsticking them. But at last her eyes opened and she saw lamplight shafting through the opening of a doorway into the room.

Instinctively she turned her head on the pillow and reached out a hand for Rowan. Shock tingled through her. He wasn't there; someone had kidnapped him from her side while she slept. Only half awake, not thinking sensibly, Ellen scrambled off the bed and ran towards the open door, reaching it just as the light went out and the room was plunged into darkness.

Unable to see anything for a few moments because her eyes weren't adjusted to the dark, she stretched out her hands before her and moved forwards hoping she would feel the door before she walked into it—and it came to her then that it wasn't the main door of the bedroom she was walking towards, it was the door of the dressing room.

So perhaps she was dreaming after all and Rowan was still in the bed behind her. Yes, that was what was happening. She was dreaming that someone had kidnapped him. The fear that Dermid might take him from her had got on her mind and she was dreaming....

'Ahh!' Her gasp of fright was spontaneous as her

hands touched not the hard wooden panelling of a door but something soft and woolly. Almost at the same time as she gasped Dermid's voice swore huskily, his favourite crisp expletive which had always shocked her puritanical mother.

'Ellen, what the hell are you doing?' he went on. 'You scared the wits out of me!'

Her hands dropped to her sides and she rubbed them nervously against her hips. Moonlight was filtering into the room now through the lace curtains. It dappled Dermid's face, limned the shape of his head and shoulders.

'I ... I ... thought I was dreaming that someone was kidnapping Rowan,' she stammered, backing away from him into a shaft of moonlight which coated her whole figure in silver. 'Where is he?' she demanded, pushing her hair back from her brow realising that her eyes hadn't deceived her. Rowan hadn't been in the bed beside her. 'What have you done with him?'

'Well, I haven't kidnapped him,' he drawled, going over to the chest of the drawers and pulling open one of the drawers, then switching on the small lamp on top of the chest so he could see what was in the drawer. 'I've put him in the cot,' he added, closing the first drawer and opening another. 'Any idea where my pyjama pants are?'

'No, of course not. I didn't unpack your case.'

'Then Bessie must have, because all my other underwear is in this drawer.' He slammed the drawer shut and opened the third one. 'Damn it, I wonder where they are?'

'Perhaps they're still in your case,' she said, her teeth chattering with the cold which was seeping into her. 'Why did you put Rowan in the cot? He doesn't like it. He wouldn't go into it earlier.'

'No?' To her surprise he had found his case. It was in the corner beside the chest of drawers and he was bending over it and opening it. 'Well, he's in it now, and went in without any complaints. They're not here. I must have forgotten to bring them.' He closed the case and put it back where he had found and turned to her. 'Are you sure he wouldn't go in it before?'

'Quite sure. That's why I put him in the bed.'

'I thought perhaps you'd put him in there to stop me from joining you,' he said, his mouth quirking sardonically.

'But ... but you're going to sleep in another room,' she muttered. She was still a little hazy with sleep. 'At least I thought you were because your case wasn't here ... or didn't seem to be here anyway. I thought you'd asked Bessie to make up another bed for you.' He was pulling off his sweater. 'Or that you'd decided to spend the night with your mistress.'

He paused in the unbuttoning of his shirt to slant her an ironic glance.

'What mistress?' he retorted calmly. 'You're my mistress. You're Mistress Dermid Craig, to use the old Scots title for a wife, and you have some damned funny ways of behaving.'

'Oh, stop pretending, Dermid,' she said, but the scorn in her voice didn't quite get across because she shivered suddenly and uncontrollably, and he noticed.

'Get back into bed,' he ordered curtly.

'No.'

'Ellen!' He moved towards her threateningly and guessing he intended to pick her up and carry her to the bed she spun round, blundered into the end of the bed, banging a shin and stubbing a toe. Biting her lip to keep back the cry of pain which rose to her lips, she hopped on one leg to the side of the bed she had been sleeping on and huddled quickly under the still warm bedclothes, hunching them round her shoulders as she sat bolt upright, staring straight ahead of her so that she couldn't see Dermid undressing.

Suddenly the light on the chest of drawers went out and by the silvery light of the moon she saw him moving along beside the bed on the other side, his bare skin striped in streaks of silver and shadow.

'Wh—what are you going to do?' she asked. Her teeth were still chattering.

'Get into bed too, of course,' he replied. 'Only one male is going to share this bed with you tonight—me. Our son can find a woman of his own to sleep with when he's old enough.'

Cool air wafted to her under the covers as he lifted them, then the bed sank down on the other side beneath his weight. He shifted about for a few seconds, tossed out one of the pillows, shifted about again, gave a sort of sighing grunt, then all was quiet.

Ellen sat hunched and tense, feeling the heat of his body radiating across the space which separated them, hearing the deep steady thud of his heart and her own heart's swift beat and fighting a longing to lie down close to him, to curl up against his warmth, warm her ice-cold toes against his muscular legs, rest her head on his chest, slide her arm about his waist....

She dropped the covers from her shoulders and slid her legs cautiously towards the edge of the bed. She couldn't stay in bed with him without wanting to be the way they used to be when they had slept together, so she had better get out and go and find somewhere else to sleep.

'Where are you going?' he rapped. He had jackknifed into a sitting position and before she could move again he lunged across the bed and caught hold of her arm. One jerk and she was down flat on her back with her legs sprawling apart and he was looming over her with one hand pressed against her shoulder, one hard knee pressed down on her thigh so that she was pinned to the bed.

'I can't sleep here with you in bed,' she quavered.

'Are we going to go through all that again?' he grated.

'Let me go,' she insisted. 'I can't stay in this bed knowing you've been with that woman this evening.'

'What woman?'

'You know very well what woman!'

'I haven't been with any woman. Why would I go and see another woman when you're here, exactly where I want you to be, in my bed?' he murmured, his hand moving on her shoulder, the fingers sliding stealthily under the edge of the neckline of her nightdress to caress the long hollow at her collarbone. Slowly his leg was moving across hers. Soon he would be on top of her and there would be no escape then.

'Dermid, stop it! Oh, what do you think I am? How can you humiliate me in this way?' she gasped.

'Humiliate you?' His voice cracked incredulously on the words and his head reared up away from her although he gave her no chance to escape. 'By God, Ellen, that's going too far, and you're asking to be humiliated by your damned unfounded accusation!' he growled deeply in his throat.

'Oh, let me go!' The cry ended abruptly as his mouth covered hers mercilessly, crushing her lips against her teeth until she tasted the tang of blood on her tongue. No longer gentle, his fingers clawed the nightdress away from her shoulder and she heard the soft hiss of fine cotton ripping. Then his fingers were probing the fullness of her breasts, sending excruciating painful yet exciting sensations tingling through her body to waken it from its long dormancy.

Afraid of yet exhilarated by the fierce passion she could feel throbbing through him, she tried to slide from beneath the weight of his heavy thighs, twisting and turning desperately. But her movements made her only more aware of the thrusting demand of his body, and slowly her body turned traitor on her, springing up in welcome.

But there was nothing harmonious in this coming together. For Ellen it was like being in a wrestling match with a stranger, for the Dermid she had married had never been like this and she was responding in spite of herself, her moans of protest becoming sighs of pleasure. It seemed that the impassioned ferocity of the struggle between them was merely a sharp spice to her appetite, increasing her own desire. Gentleness had gone by the board for both of them. They scratched and pinched, bit and nibbled each other in their desperate need.

'Now, I dare you to accuse me of being with another woman this evening,' whispered Dermid thickly, his breath hot against her throat, his tousled hair filling her nostrils with its strange musky smell, his hard chest crushing her breasts. He raised his head again and she saw the whites of his eyes glint in the moonlight. 'Do you honestly believe I could be like this with you if I had?' he demanded hoarsely. 'Do you, Ellen, do you?'

'I don't know. I don't know you any more. You're different,' she groaned, helplessly twisting her head from side to side on the pillow while her body, deluged by the flood of sheer sensations which was sweeping through it, pressed even more eagerly against him.

'You've changed too,' he said more softly. 'We're

strangers to each other, and it isn't surprising after nearly three years. But we won't be strangers for much longer.... Oh, Ellen,' he gasped on a long tortured breath.

'Dermid ... please,' she whispered, as suddenly fiercely demanding as he was, and thrusting her hands through his hair she gripped his head to draw it down towards her, and this time when his lips touched her offered ones it was in tender, sensual appreciation so that it didn't matter any more that they had hurt each other and had fought. Now they were partners again, but in a new dance, both of them moving in passionate sensuous rhythm towards a joyous climax.

CHAPTER FIVE

ELLEN awoke abruptly, feeling cold. Rolling over without opening her eyes, she sought instinctively with spreading arms and legs the warmth which had enveloped her all night, but found only the cold bareness of the sheet which covered the mattress and an even colder creased out-of-place pillow. There was no one in the bed with her.

Opening her eyes, she sat up. Sunless daylight shafted into the room. Mirrors on dressing table and in the wardrobe door glinted at one another icily as if in disgust at what they were reflecting; a tangle-haired nude woman lying on a bed from which the covers had slipped off to lie in a heap on the floor.

Ellen covered her face with her hands so that she couldn't see either the slim bare treacherous body or the reflections of it. Her first waking thought had been right. Someone had slept with her during the night, the first time she had had company in bed for nearly three years. Oh, yes, Dermid had been with her all right. There was nothing imaginary about the blisters on her lips or the bruises and scratch marks on her skin. Her hands slid down from her face, down over her throat and breasts, and she smiled a faintly feline smile of smug satisfaction. She could bet Dermid had a few bruises and scratches too! It had been a violent, snarling, bruising yet highly satisfactory mating.

Mating? She shuddered suddenly and goosepimples stood out all over her skin. Once again her hands went to her face, to clench against her mouth as she stared sideways at her reflection in the wardrobe mirror, seeing her eyes wide pools of green light between long curling black lashes staring back at her in apprehension. What had she done? What if she should become pregnant as a result of last night? How could she have been such a fool as to let desire overcome her reason? How could she have behaved with such wild abandon as to forget the need for protection?

Well, nothing was to be gained by worrying about it now. What was done was done, and if another child was conceived as a result of last night's passionate and fulfilling consummation of the strange love-hate relationship which existed between herself and Dermid now she would have to deal with it later. It would all depend on what he had in mind. It would all depend on whether he was going to divorce her so that he could marry someone else. Ann Menteith or her daughter Morag. . . .

'Ohh!' Ellen gagged on the jealousy which surged in her like sickness and jumping from the bed she grabbed her warm dressing-gown of green brushed nylon from the chair and wrapped it around her, tying the belt tightly at her waist. She stepped into her matching fluffy green slippers and glanced at her watch which was on the bedside table. Surprise rippled through her when she saw the time. She picked the watch up, twisting it this way and that, sure that she had made a mistake. No. It was ten-twenty-five. Then where was Rowan? Why wasn't he up and about?

Fear tingled along her nerves and she stumbled over the fallen bedclothes in her haste to get to the dressing room, all sorts of stories about 'crib' deaths whirling through her mind. Surely Rowan was too old and too healthy to die like that? Surely it happened only to very young infants, that strange stopping of life in the night?

Her breath came out in a sigh of relief when she saw that the big cot was empty. Rowan's pyjamas were lying in a heap on the floor and the jumpsuit, socks and shoes and parka he had been wearing the day before had gone. He must have got up, dressed himself and gone downstairs, probably in search of food. But why hadn't he tried to wake her first?

She knew why, she thought, as she strode back into the bedroom, noting that Dermid's corduroys, checked shirt and sweater had gone too. Dermid had woken to Rowan's rousing voice, had dressed him and taken him downstairs. He had done it without disturbing her, deliberately. It was all part of his plan to undermine her relationship with her child.

She paused at the dressing table to run a comb through the tangled curls of her hair, then slipped on a pair of nylon panties under her dressing gown. On her way to the door she picked up the torn cotton shift which had been her nightdress and felt a shiver compounded of dread and delight go through her when she saw the way it had been ripped, remembering the sound of the material tearing when Dermid had clawed it from her.

Oh, how he had changed, she thought, as she went out on to the landing. He wasn't the young man she had fallen in love with, whose eagerness to mate with her had been tempered by tenderness and love, who had always shown reverence and respect when he had made love to her as if she were some goddess at whose feet he had worshipped. Now, he was a hard-eyed, sharp-tongued, mocking devil intent only on achieving his own satisfaction and pleasure, taking what he considered to be his by right because they were married, not caring whether it was to her satisfaction and pleasure and turning away from her when it was done to fall asleep straight away, leaving her with the feeling that she had been used in spite of the heady, rapturous delight she had experienced.

Click-clack, click-clack went her heelless slippers on the stairs, echoing through the silence of the house. The lounge was empty and cold-looking, the study was dusty from yesterday's fire and in the dining room the bare polished table was not set for a meal; only the centrepiece of tawny chrysanthemums and purple michaelmas daisies were reflected in the reddish brown gloss of the wood.

Out in the hallway Ellen paused and listened, but she could hear no voices, no high treble and no deep baritone sounds. So she went in the direction of the kitchen, pushing open the door and entering into its warm, food-smelling atmosphere, sure that she would find Rowan there. But Bessie was the only person in the room, standing at the big scrubbed table rolling pastry for the pies she was making.

'Ach, ye gave me a fright, so ye did,' said Bessie. 'There was me thinking ye were having a nice lie-in this morning, having the rest Mr Dermid was telling me ye were needing....'

'Bessie, where is Rowan?' said Ellen, interrupting. 'Have you seen him?'

'Aye, I have that. He's away to Auchinshaws with his dad,' replied the housekeeper as she trimmed excess pastry off a pie. 'And you needn't fash y'rself about the laddie. He had a good breakfast—porridge, bacon and eggs, and some Ribena to drink. It did my heart good to see him eat.'

'But he doesn't like porri....' Ellen broke off and shrugged. What was the use of saying that Rowan didn't like the food Bessie had said he had eaten? He'd eaten it, and that was proof he did like it. Or had it been a case of him not daring to refuse when watched by the eagle eyes of his father?

'Auchinshaws is the Mackinnon farm, isn't it?' she asked, walking over to the table with her hands pushed into the pockets of her dressing gown.

'That's so. He's gone to see his grandma.' Bessie turned away to put the two pies she had made in the Aga cooker behind her.

'Have they gone in the Rolls?'

'Ach, no. Now why would they be going in that?' queried Bessie, going to the sink to fill the kettle with water.

'It's a long way from here.'

'Only about three or four miles through the woods and it's a good day for walking, quite mild and still, although I wouldn't be at all surprised if we didn't have rain later. The glass is down this morning, so it is. Now, why don't ye sit down, Mrs Craig, and I'll cook ye some breakfast. I was going to bring it up to you in an hour or so.'

'Just instant coffee and toast will do,' said Ellen. 'And I'll make it myself if you're busy.'

'Ye'll do no such thing,' retorted Bessie, her pale eyes flashing. 'I'm not having anyone messing about in my kitchen. Coffee and toast!' Her plump face creased in a grimace of disgust. 'What sort of a breakfast is that for anyone? It's no wonder you're as thin as a rake. Ye'll have porridge and bacon and eggs like that bairn of yours did....'

'No, no ... I couldn't.' Ellen's hands went to her stomach as it heaved at the thought of the food. 'Please, I would rather not. And there isn't time. I must go over to Auchinshaws too. What time did they leave?'

Maybe I could catch up with them. It's too far for Rowan to walk all the way and his father doesn't realise he's only a little boy....'

'Ach, the laddie will be fine. His dad will know how to look after him,' asserted Bessie. 'If he gets tired I daresay Mr Dermid will give him a piggyback. They've been gone a good hour and you don't want to be going after them. They'll be back in time for dinner about one o'clock....'

But Ellen didn't wait to hear any more. Swinging through the kitchen door, she hurried back along the passage to the hall. She must go after Rowan. She mustn't let Dermid take him away from her. And what about seeing the lawyer? Had Dermid forgotten that was why she had come, to hear the reading of that part of his grandfather's will that applied to Rowan? She must find that letter and read it again, show it to him when she caught up with him in the woods, ask him why he wasn't doing anything about it, why he hadn't told her that the main part of the will had been read already, insist that....

About to rush up the stairs, Ellen paused with a foot on the bottom step because someone was coming down, a tall woman dressed in a tweed suit and whose silvery blonde hair glimmered like a soft light in the shadows of the stairway.

'Mrs Craig? I'm Dr Menteith. I was talking to Dermid at the pier yesterday.' The voice was soft with just the slightest suspicion of a Highland lilt to it and the blue eyes were critical as they roved over Ellen's dressing gown. There was no doubt in Ellen's mind that Dr Ann Menteith regarded her as a slattern because she was still in night attire at this time of the morning. What would she think if she knew there was no nightdress under the dressing gown? What if she knew what had happened to that nightdress? Ellen dragged her wildly wandering thoughts back from last night's happenings and drawing herself up to her full height returned the blue gaze steadily.

'Yes, I remember,' she said coolly.

'Is your little boy about? I was wondering if I could look at his tongue,' said the doctor. 'I'm told he lisps rather badly and that perhaps....'

'Who told you?' demanded Ellen, suspicion flashing through her mind. Had Dermid seen this woman yesterday evening after all? Had he lied to her when he had said he hadn't been with another woman? Dermid with this cool, blue-eyed frump of a woman? No, she couldn't believe it.

'Miss Craig mentioned it to me just now. Apparently his father's tongue was tied at one time and sometimes the problem runs in a family.'

'Oh yes ... of course.' Perhaps it was the daughter after all that Dermid was interested in. Was Morag tall, too, and fair-haired, lovely in her late adolescence, a white rosebud waiting to be picked? They said, didn't they, that adolescents were sweet and acquiescent and that was why older men fell for them? Ellen came aware that Ann Menteith was staring at her in puzzlement and once more had to gather her straying thoughts together. 'I'm afraid Rowan isn't here right now. He ... he's with Derm ... my husband,' she substituted the word husband with a sort of desperate defiance. Might as well let Ann Menteith know that she was still married to Dermid and still regarded him as being married to her.

'In the garden? Or on the shore, perhaps?' suggested Ann, raising her eyebrows.

'No, no. They've gone over to Auchinshaws,' said Ellen quickly. 'And they won't be back until dinnertime.'

'Then I'll see them there,' said Ann with a complacent smile curving her thin-lipped mouth. 'I'm going there next. Old Mr Mackinnon isn't feeling so well today. While I'm there I'll examine the boy's tongue and tell Dermid about his aunt's condition. I've no doubt he'll let you know what should be done about the child's lisp when he returns later. Good morning, Mrs Craig. I'll let myself out by the side door. I know my way about the house very well.'

Ellen could have gnashed her teeth and stamped her foot in irritation. How foolish of her to tell the doctor of Dermid's and Rowan's whereabouts. Now she would have to go over to Auchinshaws as soon as she could. She ran up the stairs to the bedroom. If she'd had any sense, she thought, she would have asked the doctor for a lift over to the farm.

Snatching her toilet bag from the dressing table, she dashed down the landing to the bathroom, had a hasty wash and hurried back to the bedroom. She flung off her dressing gown and, bra-less, pulled on a thin cotton T-shirt. From the wardrobe she took out dark green velour pants and stepped into them. A V-necked velour sweater which matched the pants went over the T-shirt and then she pulled on suede rubber-soled running shoes. She would jog through the woods as she often jogged in the early morning in Ottawa. The exercise would do her good, calm her nerves and make her ready to confront Dermid again.

When she was dressed she combed her hair again and applied make-up, putting on more of the cinnamon-coloured lipstick than usual to hide the marks on her lips. Then she picked up her handbag, unzipped it and took out the envelope containing the lawyer's letter.

She read the letter more carefully than she had done when she had first received it and realised rather ruefully that she had missed some words. She was requested to be at Inchcullin House the *week beginning* October the thirty-first and not *on* that specific date as she had assumed, which meant that any day of this week would have done and she need not have come straight here yesterday. The letter went on to say that her presence was necessary in accordance with Neil Craig's wishes for the reading of the *part* of his will which dealt with his great-grandson Rowan Maxwell Craig.

Relieved that she had cleared up that little mystery, Ellen studied the heading of the letter. The lawyers Scott, Murray and MacCleggan had their offices in Portcullin and the letter had been signed by Wallace Scott. Perhaps it would be a good idea to phone Mr Scott and inform him that she was here, and make an appointment to see him. Yes, that was what she would do while Dermid was out of the house. There was no need for her to wait for him to take action. She could arrange this for herself ... for Rowan's sake.

In a few minutes she was downstairs and in the study leafing through the local telephone directory. It didn't take long for her to find the number of the lawyer's office and soon she was speaking to his secretary, who told her in a soft lilting voice that Mr Scott would be pleased to talk with her.

'Mr Scott, this is Ellen Craig,' Ellen went into the attack as soon as he announced himself. 'You wrote to me concerning Neil Craig's will and asked me to be present at Inchcullin House some time this week.'

'Ach, just so, just so, Mrs Craig.' His voice was

slow and fruity and she had an image of a large, fat man. 'And did you have a good flight over?'

Ellen gritted her teeth, forcing herself to be patient and go through the usual polite preliminaries.

'Yes, thank you,' she said politely. 'Mr Scott, I haven't much time and I would like to meet you as soon as possible to hear the part of Mr Craig's will which applies to my son.'

'Well now,' the slow drawling voice made Ellen itch with impatience. 'Have you discussed this matter with your husband, Mr Dermid Craig?'

'I ... er ... no ... at least not yet.'

'Then I think you should do that, Mrs Craig, and then both of you should come and see me. He can tell you all the details of the will. He has a copy of it there.'

'But ... but ... in your letter to me you said that my presence was requested for the reading of that part of the will, and I thought you would be doing that either in your office or here in Inchcullin House.'

'Aye, just so.' Mr Scott took a long wheezy breath. 'But you see, Mrs Craig, the wording in that letter isn't mine. and I think it best if you discuss the whole matter with your husband first and then if there's any legal difficulty over the execution of the will you can both come and see me.'

'But....'

'I'm sorry, Mrs Craig, but I'll have to ring off now. There is another client waiting to see me. Don't forget now, come and see me with your husband if there is any problem, and we'll do our best to solve it. Good day to you, now.'

Mr Scott for all his slow speech was very quick when it came to putting down a telephone receiver, thought Ellen, as she heard the line go dead before she had even time to reply to his pleasant 'Good day' and she had the uneasy feeling that she had been brushed off, that she was a person he didn't particularly want to know about.

Then why had he written asking her to come here? *The wording in the letter isn't mine*, he had said. Then whose was it? Who would have the right to dictate such a letter and have it sent out in the lawyer's name? Only someone closely connected with the execution of Neil Craig's will—and it was easy to guess from Mr Scott's constant suggestion that she should discuss the matter of the will first with her husband who the person was. The wording in the letter was Dermid's. He knew what was in the part of the will applying to Rowan. He was one of the executors of the will and she could do nothing until she had discussed it with him.

Then the sooner she saw him again the better. Ellen strode across to the study door and pulled it open. Instead of jogging over to Auchinshaws she would get James to drive her there in the Rolls. Down the passage she went to the kitchen.

'Ach, so there you are,' said Bessie, looking up. 'I've made coffee and there are some fresh baps hot from the oven for ye. Ye can have them with some of me home-made marmalade. It's all there for ye, on the table.'

The smell of the coffee and hot bread rolls was too much for Ellen. She was hungry, she realised, and so she gave in and sat down at the end of the table which Bessie had set with a neat hand-embroidered cloth and took one of the baps from the basket.

'There now, that's more sensible,' said Bessie approvingly, coming across with the coffee pot and pouring some into a mug. 'If I let you go out without anything to eat Mr Dermid would have something to say to me. "Make a good breakfast for Mrs Craig," he says to me, "and take it up to her." As it is he isn't going to be at all pleased when he knows ye didn't have y'r breakfast in bed.' Bessie sat down and picked up the mug of coffee which she had poured for herself and gave Ellen a sharp assessing glance. 'Ye could do worse, ye know,' she added.

'Do worse? What do you mean?' countered Ellen, who was just a little shaken by Bessie's report of Dermid's concern for her welfare.

'For a husband. It isn't every man who would let his wife take a job three thousand odd miles away from where his home is. Ye can think yourself lucky he hasn't divorced ye.'

'It isn't really any of your business, is it,' retorted Ellen stiffly, rising to her feet.

'No, I suppose it isn't, but I never was one for keeping me thoughts to meself,' said Bessie honestly.

'Is James about?' asked Ellen coolly.

'Now what would ye be wanting him for?'

'To drive me over to Auchinshaws.'

'Ye're out of luck. He's away to Portcullin in the car. Its engine is due for a change of oil so he won't be back until this afternoon. But there isn't much point in ye going over to the farm, Mr Dermid should be back soon. . . .'

'Bessie, when I want your advice I'll ask for it,' said Ellen through her teeth. 'Thank you for the coffee and baps. Both were delicious. And now I'm going through the woods to Auchinshaw. All right?'

'Suit yourself,' said the housekeeper with a lift of her shoulders. 'But don't get lost, will ye?'

How could she possibly get lost in these woods? thought Ellen crossly as she jogged gently along the well marked path which wound between the trees. It wasn't as if they were the Canadian bush, thick and tangled. All she had to do was follow this path and sooner or later she would come out at the other side of the forest and look down into the valley where the farm was situated.

In contrast to the previous afternoon the air was damp and mild with just a hint of drizzling rain in it. Nothing moved amongst the trees whose bluish-green needles were spangled with drops of moisture. There was a smell of rotting vegetation and the silence was almost tangible, heavy and thick. No birds were singing and even the stream was quiet.

After a while jogging became difficult because the path narrowed and sloped more steeply uphill. Jagged rocks appeared through the carpet of pine needles and crushed wet birch leaves—ankle-turners, Ellen called them, designed especially to bring down the unwary jogger or walker. So she went more slowly and carefully, thinking over what she would say to Dermid when she saw him, and as she walked she was aware that the rain was falling more steadily and was glad she was under the shelter of the trees.

The path widened out again leading into a glade, a grassy clearing in the trees. Ellen paused and looked round, hearing the pattering of raindrops. There seemed to be two paths leading out of the glade. Which was the one to Auchinshaws? Her brow furrowed with the effort as she tried to remember which one she had taken with Dermid when they had come this way five years ago, and failed.

She looked at her watch. Quarter past twelve already. If Dermid intended to be back at Inchcullin for one o'clock dinner he must have left Auchinshaws by now and be coming this way. Poor little Rowan! How his legs must be aching after walking there and having to walk back without much of a rest in between.

She should turn back to Inchcullin or should she choose one of the paths and go on hoping to meet the other two? She decided to go on and choosing the right-hand path guessing that the other one would take her down to the sea shore, she pulled the hood of her velour sweater up over her already damp hair and set off, hands in her pockets.

She had been walking for about fifteen minutes, noticing that the path was winding downhill, when she saw Dermid come round a bend and start up the slope towards her.

'Hi,' she called. 'Where's Rowan?'

He lifted his head in surprise but didn't stop walking, and in a few seconds was beside her. Raindrops glistened on his hair and the shoulders of his fawn golf jacket were dark with damp.

'What are you doing out here in this downpour?' he demanded, deliberately evading her question, she thought.

'Coming over to Auchinshaws to get Rowan. Where is he?'

'I've left him with my mother for the rest of the day,' he replied coolly.

'You had no right!' she said hotly. 'Oh, I might have known you'd do something like that!' And swinging away from him she would have set off down the path again if he hadn't caught hold of her arm and dragged her back, pulling her close against him. His eyes were dark yet glittery, his mouth taut, and he spoke softly and threateningly.

'I have as much right to leave him with *my* mother as you have to leave him with *yours,* and you're not going to get him. You're going to walk back to Inchcullin with me. Unlike you, I haven't a whole week off work, but only two days, today and tomorrow, and during that time I hope to get things settled between us. Ellen, we can't go on as we are.'

'Wh—wh—what do you mean?' she asked, stalling for time, knowing very well what he meant.

'I mean we have to decide whether we want to stay married to each other,' he said bluntly.

They stared at each other in silence while the rain fell with a soft sibilance through the branches of the trees. Was it to end here, wondered Ellen, on this sad November day, that dream which had begun so gladly one golden summer's day, five years ago? No, no, not yet, something inside her whispered. Play for time.

'Is ... is there someone else?' she forced the words through dry lips, 'someone you would prefer to be married to?'

Dark lashes drifted down over his eyes. He let go of her arm and half turned away from her.

'It's beginning to rain pretty hard,' he said. 'Let's get back to the house.'

He started to walk on and Ellen stood there undecided as ever, torn between following him and going on to Auchinshaws to rescue her child.... To rescue her child from what? The bad influence of Kate Mackinnon?

'Ellen.' Dermid's voice was quiet but authoritative. 'He'll be all right, honestly. He'll go collecting eggs with her this afternoon and meet the animals. We'll pick him up later, drive over in the Rolls when James brings it back, maybe stay to tea. Mother would like to see you. A few hours together without him distracting our attention is all we need.'

'Your mother's suggestion?' she queried with a lift of her eyebrows, deliberately recalling the time when he had accused her of being under her mother's influence.

'No, all my own idea,' he replied with a mocking quirk of his mouth.

'Like the wording in the letter Mr Scott the lawyer sent to me?'

He came a few steps back along the path, a frown darkening his face.

'Now what are you getting at?' he demanded.

'I phoned Mr Scott this morning to make an appointment to see him since he had written to me saying my presence was necessary here for Rowan's sake, and he told me that the wording in that letter wasn't his.'

'So?'

'So I guessed it was yours.'

'And ...?'

'And I'm beginning to think you've tricked me into coming here and bringing Rowan by getting Mr Scott to write instead of writing to me yourself.'

'All right, I admit it—I had to find some way to see Rowan. Writing to you and asking you to bring him didn't work. All I've ever received from you are those stiff little notes saying he's perfectly happy and so are you and the job is fine, just fine, and you're busy, busy with no time to fly over on a visit right now.' He mimicked her way of speaking with a mockery which made her flinch. 'God knows,' he went on roughly, 'I've been patient enough with you, waiting and hoping you'd come over to stay for a while at Kilruddock....'

'I couldn't, I couldn't,' she interrupted him. 'I couldn't come and stay in that house.'

'Why the hell not? What's wrong with it? You furnished it. I haven't changed a thing.'

'I couldn't come ... not after I'd heard about ... about ... that girl in the typing pool,' she stuttered through stiff lips. 'Not after I'd heard you ... you'd been unfaithful to me,' she added. It was out at last and she stood facing him, head up, eyes direct, and waiting tensely for his answer.

'You heard what?' he questioned, his brow wrinkling in puzzlement. 'Who told you that?'

'Sheila Moffatt, my mother's cousin.'

'When?' He was frowning again and his eyes were glittering like jet in his suddenly pale face.

'When she visited us in Ottawa at Christmas nearly two years ago.'

'And you believed her.' His mouth took on a bitter curve.

'It was hard not to, especially when you didn't come, especially when you didn't write.'

Dermid swore vehemently and wiped away the drops of water which had begun to run down his face from his wet hair with the back of one hand.

'My God, you listened to that loose-tongued troublemaker and you believed what she said?' he rasped. 'Don't you know she's always hated my guts because I've got in the way of her beloved son? Every chance she has she spreads lies about me!'

'She said you'd been giving lifts to a girl from the typing pool regularly.'

'To Nancy Cowan, that's right. But what was wrong in doing that? It happened only when she missed the bus and I'd come across her waiting at the bus-stop at the end of the street. It seemed callous to go by when I knew she was going the same way that I was. Don't tell me you've never had a lift to work in your boss's car, because I know differently.'

'But Sheila said there was more to it than that. She said the girl used to talk about her association with you in the women's washrooms and that it was known she'd spent the night ... in our ... in the house with you, that she'd been seen leaving the house with you in the mornings.'

If anything his face had gone paler and the muscles along his jaw tensed as he struggled to control his anger.

'God knows I'm not a saint and never have been,' he rasped, 'but do you really think I would conduct an affair with a juvenile typist in my own backyard under the noses of my neighbours, my relatives and employers? Come on, Ellen, give me credit for more subtlety than that! Nancy was never in our house, and I can't help it if she giggled about me with her adolescent friends in the washroom. I gave her lifts for a few weeks only when I went to Colombia for three months.' His dark glance taunted her. 'I found the *señoritas* there much more fascinating.'

Ellen clenched her hands in the pockets of her sweater and her glance wavered away from his. Was it possible what he said about Sheila was true? That her mother's cousin had spread lies about him out of spite because he had been appointed to a senior position in the company over her son's head?

'There's rarely smoke without fire,' she muttered.

'Meaning you don't trust me,' he accused.

'I've tried to.' The confrontation was beginning to sap her strength and her legs were trembling.

'But not for long.' His eyes narrowed and he gave her a bitter glance. 'I'm finding it hard to take, Ellen, that the only reason you haven't brought Rowan to see me is because your mother's cousin implied I was having an affair with that typist. You're just using what she said as an excuse to cover up some other reason, aren't you?'

'What other reason?'

'Another man. Someone with whom you've been

having an affair?' His mouth curved cynically. 'A wife is as capable of being unfaithful as a husband, you know. And you've had plenty of opportunities over the past two and half years.'

'I have not!' she spat the words out at him furiously, her cheeks aflame with indignation.

'Expect me to believe you?' he drawled mockingly.

'Oh!' For a moment she was speechless with offended pride. He hadn't denied he'd been unfaithful, she noticed with bitterness. He had only denied he'd had an affair with the typist. 'If you'd really wanted to see Rowan you'd have come to Ottawa,' she stormed, finding her voice again. 'But you didn't come. You didn't care enough about him or me to neglect your job and come to see us, so why should you assume I'd neglect my job to bring him to see you?'

He was silent, staring at her with eyes which had a strained look about them. Again he wiped the rain from his face with the back of his hand, still staring at her thoughtfully, then again his mouth curved bitterly.

'I didn't come because I had this impression that I wasn't wanted any more,' he said harshly and flatly, 'because you'd discovered that marriage wasn't what you wanted after all and you preferred to be liberated.' Scorn made his voice even harsher. 'I can think of no better way to turn a man off, can you, Ellen?' he challenged bleakly. 'And those skimpy cold little notes of yours certainly had that effect on me. To hell with you, I was damned if I was going to run after a woman who'd made it obvious she could manage very well without me.'

'Well, what about your letters!' she retorted defensively, but couldn't go on because her voice was trembling. She was shaking from head to foot, not so much with the cold dampness which was chilling her to the marrow but more with the sheer misery which was stealthily creeping over her as a result of this confrontation. And the rain was increasing, slanting down between them.

'What's the matter with you?' demanded Dermid, his eyes narrowing, their glance drifting over her face and stopping at her mouth. 'Are you ill?'

'No. I ... I'm just cold, th-that's all,' she stuttered.

'That's not surprising. We're getting soaked standing here.' He raised a hand and touched her lips where they were bruised. It was a finger-tip touch, hardly a caress, but it had the effect of rooting her to the spot with amazement. 'Did I do that?' he asked softly, still staring at her mouth. 'Did I bruise your lips last night?'

'Who else?' she countered, hoping the words would come out sharply and cuttingly, but she was shivering too much and could speak only in a choked whisper.

'I'm glad I did.' He spoke with a sort of soft viciousness and something hot and red came and went in the tawny darkness of his eyes, before he turned away from her abruptly. 'Come on,' he added in a more normal voice as he glanced at his watch. 'Let's go back to the house before we're drowned in this deluge.'

Without waiting to see whether Ellen followed he set off up the path again and she watched him disappear into the rain-misted greenish gloom of the woods. Now he had gone she could go on to Auchinshaws and get Rowan, but something in her shrank suddenly from facing Dermid's mother on her own. She had a feeling Kate Mackinnon would be critical of her both as a wife and a mother and would say so if Dermid wasn't there. And anyway, she could hardly go on, soaked as she was. It would be easier and more sensible to go back to Inchcullin House, to change into day clothing and go later to the farm in the Rolls with Dermid. Besides, she had yet to find out from Dermid what was in his grandfather's will for Rowan.

That was why she was turning back and following Dermid, she assured herself as she began to walk back up the path, and not because he had insisted she should go back. She was going back for Rowan's sake in the same way she had come for Rowan's sake, and once she had found out what was in the will she would pack her and his bags and leave as soon as she could, go and stay with Sheila Moffatt.

She didn't catch up with Dermid and there was no sign of him when she reached the house. As she went in by the side door she heard the phone ringing in the study. There was no one about in the hall and she hesitated, listening to the phone bell's imperative summons. No one seemed to be coming to answer it, so she made her way to the room and reaching the desk picked up the receiver.

'Hello, this is Inchcullin House,' she said.

'Oh ... hello ...' The voice was female and youthful. 'Is that Mrs Blair, the housekeeper?'

'No. Do you want to speak to her?'

'No. I wondered if.... Is Dermid there, Mr Dermid Craig?'

'I'll go and fetch him for you. May I tell him who is calling?'

'It's Morag. Morag Menteith,' said the voice.

Ellen held the receiver away from her ear and glared at it as jealousy ripped maliciously through her. She was very tempted to clang the receiver back on its rest, but at that moment the study door swung open and Dermid came in. He had changed his clothes and was wearing well-tailored fawn pants and a brown and gold striped leisure shirt.

'Is it for me?' he queried, coming over and holding out his hand for the receiver. 'I'm expecting a call.'

Slowly Ellen handed the receiver over, hoping that her feelings, the deadly corrosive jealousy, wasn't showing in her face.

'Yes, it's for you,' she said, and went from the room, her wet running shoes squelching on the floor.

She closed the study door firmly behind her, resisting the temptation to linger outside and listen to the conversation she would hear. Once she had eavesdropped on a conversation in Ottawa and today she had learned that what she had heard could have been lies told out of spite. So never again would she listen in.

Upstairs she went, to change her clothes. The bed had been made and the room had been tidied—by Bessie, she supposed. But Dermid had left his wet trousers and discarded shirt and sweater in a heap on the floor. Automatically she picked them up and found hangers for the pants and shirt and hung them outside the wardrobe so that they would dry without creasing too much.

She changed out of her wet velour suit, hung that up and looked for other clothes to wear. Another skirt, made from Arran tartan, all pinks, greys and dark reds gathered softly into a waistband, long and flattering to the length of her thighs and legs and to the slimness of her ankles. With it a shirt of fine wool, strawberry pink in colour, smocked across the shoulder saddle. High-heeled black sandals completed the outfit and she thought she looked elegant and sophisticated, far too sophisticated to be disturbed by the sound of a young woman's voice asking to speak to Dermid.

But she was disturbed and she was wishing she hadn't heard that soft slightly breathless voice, wishing she hadn't heard him say on a note of satisfaction that he had been expecting a call at that time. He had been expecting Morag to phone him and that was why he had hurried on to Inchcullin House leaving her in the woods after telling Ellen he wasn't in love with her any more.

For that was what he had meant, wasn't it, when he had said she had turned him off? And it had hurt her far more deeply than she had expected to be told something she had suspected for some time. Why? Staring at her reflection with wide green eyes, Ellen groaned. Had she fallen in love with him again? Or was it possible she had never fallen out of love with him?

CHAPTER SIX

ALTHOUGH it wasn't long since she had eaten breakfast and she wasn't feeling hungry there was no possibility of Ellen avoiding the usual midday dinner. When she went downstairs Agnes was in the hall on her way to the dining room and immediately suggested that Ellen accompany her there.

The oval mahogany table was set with its usual formality even though it was a weekday. Lace table mats were crisp and white against the glossy wood, and silver cutlery gleamed softly in the rain-grey dimness of the room. Dermid wasn't there and Bessie had already placed bowls of steaming broth on the table before he came in to take his seat.

He was frowning as if something had displeased him and, as he shook out his table napkin, he gave Ellen a sharp underbrowed glance and she felt her nerves quiver in reaction. What had she done now? she wondered. Oh, why was she so on edge when she was with him? Why couldn't she ignore him?

Agnes was in a chatty mood, which was just as well, thought Ellen, as having eaten only a few spoonfuls of the broth she toyed with a large helping of shepherd's pie and vegetables. She and Dermid were hardly scintillating. Apart from a few grunts, which he made presumably to assure Agnes that there was someone else at the table with her, he was withdrawn and silent.

His thoughts were taken up by the person to whom he had been speaking, perhaps? By Morag Menteith? Again Ellen felt jealousy surge through her and her fork clattered against her plate as she put it down. She couldn't eat another thing. She had to get away, leave the house as soon as she could. She couldn't stay any longer knowing Dermid was involved with Ann Menteith's daughter.

'Ellen!' Agnes's voice was quite sharp for her. 'I've asked you three times now. Did Dr Menteith look at Rowan's tongue?'

'Oh,' Ellen wiped her mouth on her napkin quickly, more to hide the startled expression on her face than for any other reason. 'I ... I'm sorry, Aunt Agnes, I was miles away. Rowan wasn't here. He'd gone to Auchinshaws with Dermid before I saw the doctor. But she said she was going to the farm too and would examine Rowan there.' She flicked a glance at Dermid. He didn't seem very interested in food either and had laid down his knife and fork and had pushed his half empty plate to one side. 'Did she arrive when you were there?'

'Yes. Ann said the tongue is slightly tied underneath and that if we'd like to take Rowan to her surgery tomorrow she'll attend to it,' he replied brusquely.

'But surely it will have to be done in hospital?' Ellen was suddenly very possessive about her son again. If anything was going to be done to his tongue she was going to make the decision about it and no one else.

'Apparently it doesn't have to be done in hospital. It can be done with a local anaesthetic by a G.P. and it won't hurt much. He'll just have to stay off solid food for a while, eat baby foods again,' replied Dermid coolly.

'I'd like someone else to do it,' Ellen said determinedly.

'For God's sake why?' He lost his temper suddenly;

his eyes glinted malevolently at her and his voice rasped harshly.

'Dermid!' protested Agnes in a fluttery voice.

'I'm sorry, Agnes,' he said, but didn't sound at all apologetic as he gave Ellen another withering glance. 'But I can't understand Ellen's attitude. Ann, as you know, is a perfectly good surgeon and knows a lot about childish ailments, and since there isn't a hospital near here such small operations can be done quite adequately in a doctor's surgery.'

'Dermid is right, dear,' said Agnes. 'Ann is a very good doctor.'

'I don't care if she is or not,' replied Ellen woodenly. 'I'd like another opinion.'

Dermid swore exasperatedly, Agnes complained again and Bessie came into the room to take away the dinner plates, tut-tutting disgustedly about the amount of food which had been left on them.

'So where are you going to get that second opinion?' asked Dermid as Bessie left the room.

'In Ottawa, of course, when Rowan and I return there,' Ellen replied coolly, refusing to look at him.

In the silence which followed her announcement Bessie reappeared with dishes of apple pie and custard which she placed in front of them. Ellen stared down at hers, wondering how she was going to even taste it, let alone eat all of it.

'If it's a second opinion you want you don't have to take Rowan back to Ottawa to get it,' said Dermid slowly. 'Dr Mackay in Kilruddock will examine him.'

'Yes, that's a good idea. He's a very good children's doctor,' said Agnes sweetly and hopefully, and Ellen clenched her hands on her knees under the table. She was becoming rather tired of Agnes's support of Dermid.

'But Rowan and I won't be going to Kilruddock,' she said as smoothly as she could. 'Once you've told me what's in the will for Rowan I'm going over to Ayr to stay with Sheila Moffatt for a few days before flying back.'

'No son of mine is going to stay in the house of that woman,' said Dermid between his teeth. 'You can go and stay with her if you like, but Rowan will stay with me at Kilruddock. I'll take him there tomorrow and arrange for Dr Mackay to look at his tongue.'

'No!'

'Why the hell shouldn't I?' His voice was harsh and Ellen heard Agnes twitter in objection. 'I'm his father, his legal guardian, and I have every right to look after him. Or is that a fact of life you've decided to forget?'

'No, it isn't. I haven't forgotten.'

'Then why won't you let me do anything for him?' he challenged. His narrowed eyes raked her critically. 'I think I know why you want a second opinion,' he drawled dryly. 'It's because you don't like Ann Menteith for some reason and not because you're really concerned for Rowan....'

'That's not true. I am concerned,' she retorted defensively.

'Really?' The lift of his eyebrows mocked her. 'Then why haven't you had his tongue seen to before this?'

'I've told you—I did. I tried.' To her intense irritation she felt a desire to burst into tears, futile tears of frustration and anger because he was taunting her and criticising her in front of Agnes. 'Oh, what do you know about it?' she flared. 'How can you know what it's like to be a parent struggling on your own to do your best for a child without any help from ... from....'

'From the other parent, isn't that what you were

going to say?' Dermid cut in, and the mockery faded from his face as leaned towards her across the corner of the table. 'Ellen, you didn't have to struggle on your own and you don't have to now,' he went on quietly. 'I'm willing to have Rowan live with me, I've always been willing to do that, but you've been so selfish, so unwilling to share him.'

'But ... but if you take him to live with you how do I know you'll let me have him back? How do I know you won't keep him?' she cried out, voicing her inmost fear.

'You'll just have to trust me, won't you?' he retorted, giving her a bitter look. 'As I've trusted you over the past couple of years, to no good purpose, apparently.'

'Dermid—Ellen,' Agnes quavered, and suddenly unable to control her feelings any more, Ellen sprang to her feet and with a muttered excuse hurried from the room.

In the hall she stood for a moment with her hand pressed against her mouth as she struggled to contain emotions which threatened to overwhelm her. What should she do now? Go and get Rowan, bring him back here? And then? She couldn't stay here, she couldn't spend another night under the same roof as Dermid, possibly in the same bed. She had to leave somehow, go somewhere else, even if it was only to stay in the hotel at Portcullin until she could go on the ferry.

Behind her Dermid's footsteps clicked sharply and authoritatively on the polished floor and, panicking, she made for the stairs. Her foot was on the bottom step, her hand was reaching for the banister when he grabbed her other arm and jerked her round roughly to face him. She wrenched her arm free of his grasp and backed away into the curved end of the banister.

'Keep your hands off me,' she said in a low furious voice. 'Don't you dare touch me again!'

'Afraid, Ellen?' he taunted softly, but he thrust his hands into his trouser pockets as if he didn't trust them. 'Afraid I might leave my mark on you as I did last night? Or afraid of your own responses?' He stepped closer to her and his breath feathered her face when he spoke again. 'You liked it last night, didn't you?' he murmured, his eyes glinting wickedly. 'And perhaps that's what this is all about. You're picking a fight with me because you want to....'

'I'm not picking a fight! It's you, with all your criticism of me.' She covered her face with her hands so that he couldn't see it. 'I couldn't stay in there to be criticised any more by you!'

There was a short silence. She waited, hoping he would move away, but he didn't, and she heard him let his breath out in a long shaky sigh.

'I'm sorry,' he said softly. 'I didn't mean to criticise you, but I'm very concerned about Rowan's future and I'd like him to have the chance to grow up in a home where there's harmony and love, so we have to find a solution to our present problem of living apart—and we're not going to do that if you lose your temper and disagree with everything I suggest.'

'You never lose your temper, I suppose,' she retorted sarcastically but shakily, lowering her hands. Dermid wasn't touching her, but he was standing as close to her as he could without and she could feel the warmth of him radiating out to her, see a pulse beating at the base of his throat left bare by the open collar of his shirt, hear the steady thud of his heart and smell the tangy wholesome scent of his skin.

'Only when I'm provoked,' he replied. 'And you

have to admit you've been very provocative, in more ways than one.'

'But why should I have to agree to everything you suggest?' she argued, leaning away from him as far as she could because physically he was overwhelming her. Her senses were beginning to reel and her legs felt weak again so that she was glad of the support of the end of the banister. 'Why don't you try doing something I suggest for a change?'

'What do you think I've been doing for the past two and a half years?' he countered.

'I didn't suggest we separate. You did,' she accused.

'But it was you who wanted to go to work in Canada and I agreed to let you do your own thing. You've never shown any desire to end the separation, so I've gone along with it—I call that agreeing with your suggestion, fitting in with what you wanted to do,' he replied quietly, and stepped back from her as he heard Bessie's footsteps, heavy and purposeful, coming along the passage from the kitchen. 'Let's go into the study,' he suggested.

'Why?'

'To look at my grandfather's will. You want to know what's in it for Rowan, don't you? And afterwards we can discuss what we should do about him,' he replied, and turning went towards the study door.

From the dining room came the sound of Bessie's voice as she exclaimed over the apple pie which hadn't been eaten, followed by Agnes's voice apologising because the food had been left. Slowly Ellen followed Dermid. It was what she had come for, the reading of the part of the will concerning Rowan, and as soon as it was done she could leave. Oh, what was the use of her planning what she should do afterwards? It would all depend on their discussion. She must try and keep her temper. She must listen to what Dermid had to say and answer reasonably. She mustn't let her emotions interfere.

A fire had been lit in the study and its flames were bright orange and yellow against the soot-blackened back of the hearth. The room was warm and cosy, especially with the door closed, a peaceful, comfortable haven in which to spend a wet afternoon browsing amongst the books Neil Craig had collected over the years or listening to his selection of records. How she wished she could lounge on the big cretonne-covered settee by the fire and forget today's problems, pretend it was five years ago and she and Dermid were only a few days married, in love, madly in love, so in love they would sit close together, arms about each other and....

Determined not to let nostalgia for what had been sway her in any way, Ellen turned her back on the settee and sat down on the edge of a straight-backed hard-seated chair near one of the lace-curtained windows, far away from the fire and in a direct draught. If she sat in the cold perhaps she would remain cool, she thought as she watched Dermid unlock a drawer in the lower part of the old rolltop desk. From the drawer he took a wide buff envelope which he opened to pull out several sheets of foolscap paper which were clipped together. Then he looked up and across at her.

'Why don't you sit by the fire?' he said, gesturing towards the settee.

'I'm all right here, thank you,' she replied stiffly. He gave her a sceptical glance, shrugged his shoulders indifferently and sat down on the settee himself, stretching his long legs before him and leaning his shoulders against the cushioned back. He looked relaxed, thoroughly at home, while she was sitting all tensed, mentally as well as physically, on edge.

'First of all, I have to tell you that Grandfather willed this house, the sixty acres of land which go with it plus his shares in Craig & Rose to me,' drawled Dermid as he turned over a foolscap page.

'I know,' said Ellen, and he looked up in surprise.

'You do? Who told you?' he asked.

'Aunt Agnes, last night.' She saw him frown irritably and added quickly in Agnes's defence, 'Oh, she wasn't gossiping. She told me when I asked her if she knew what was in the will. You see, I was under the impression that the whole will hadn't been read and couldn't be read until Rowan and I were present.' She paused and gave him a searching glance. 'You wanted me to have that impression, didn't you? Why?'

'Because I wanted you to come here,' he replied coolly, seemingly intent on studying what was written on one of the pages he was holding. 'Would you like to read all of it?'

'No, thank you. Only the part concerning Rowan interests me.'

'You could come and sit over here and look over my shoulder while I read it to you,' he suggested.

'I would rather stay here,' she replied stiffly, and felt her face flush warmly when he gave her a derisive glance. He had been right when he had said she was afraid of her own responses to his physical presence, and the fact that he knew it gave him an advantage over her in this tug-of-war game they were playing; a power which he would have no hesitation in using if he could, so she was going to stay as far away from him as she could.

'Ellen.' The sound of her name spoken persuasively yet a little mockingly as if her behaviour amused him made her quiver. Turning on the chair, she looked out of the window. The rain had stopped and in the west the clouds were lifting. A band of silvery sunlight glittered on the dark sea close to the horizon, promise of better weather to come.

'Read it—oh, read it and get it over and done with!' Ellen exclaimed in a strangled voice. 'And then Rowan and I can leave.'

The short silence which followed her outburst was broken only by the crackling of the fire and the ticking of the grandfather clock. Ellen continued to stare out of the window. She guessed that Dermid was staring at her, and she expected him to make some retort, but when he did speak it was to read from the will, coldly and without expression. The language was surprisingly simple and she had no difficulty in understanding Neil Craig's bequest to his great-grandson. He had left a large amount of money in trust for Rowan which the boy would inherit when he was twenty-one years of age. Until that date a proportion of the money could be used, at the discretion of the three trustees named, for the purpose of Rowan's education, provided he lived and went to school in Scotland.

Dermid stopped reading and Ellen swung round in the chair to look across the room at him.

'Is that all?' she asked.

'Yes.' The papers rustled as he arranged them in order again.

'But ... but ... Mr Scott could have told me all that in the letter he sent,' she objected. Then when Dermid didn't even look at her or make any explanation she demanded suspiciously, 'Who are the trustees?'

'Wallace Scott, you and myself,' he replied. 'That's why I wanted you to come, so we could discuss Rowan's future.'

'I don't believe it!' she exclaimed, jumping to her feet and going over to stand in front of him. 'I don't believe he has to live and go to school in this country before any of that money can be used for his education. I don't believe your grandfather would make such a condition.'

'Somehow I didn't think you'd believe it,' he drawled, wearily exasperated.

'It's your idea, isn't it?' she accused hotly. 'You suggested it to your grandfather so you could get control of Rowan, so you could take him from me and....'

'It is not my idea,' he broke in furiously. 'I had nothing to do with it. My grandfather was quite capable of thinking for himself right up to the time of his death. He had his own ideas on how he wanted his money used after he'd gone.' He gave her a bitter glance. 'He had his own ideas on marriage too and, I can tell you now, he didn't think much of the way in which you and I are managing ours.' He drew a deep breath and tilted his head back against the back of the couch. Through downward-drooping eyelashes he studied her and his mouth curved upwards in one corner in a slight smile.

'Since you don't believe not only anything I tell you but also what I've read to you, you'd better read the will for yourself and then perhaps you'll believe in that condition,' he drawled, but he made no move to hand the sheaf of papers to her.

'All right,' she agreed, and held out her hand.

'Sit down here and I'll show you where to start reading,' he suggested slowly, and now there was a sort of insolent speculation in the way he was looking at her, in the way his glance rested on the low fastening of her blouse where the hollow of her breasts was just showing as she leaned forward, and she straightened up quickly.

'No, I don't want to sit down,' she replied. 'Give me the will.'

'Weren't you ever taught to say please?' he taunted.

'Dermid, stop fooling about and let me have it!'

He moved then, but not to offer her the will. One hand reached up to grasp her held-out hand, fingers closing bruisingly about hers.

'Let go!' she cried, trying to pull free, but with a sharp jerk Dermid pulled her forward and losing balance she fell on top of him, sprawling in an ungainly fashion, hearing the paper on which the will was written crackling beneath her, feeling the pressure of his knee between hers. The breath jolted out of her as she came into contact with his hard body and she lay helplessly reaching out with her hands to the back of the settee to push against it so she could stand up again.

'Mmm, you smell sweet and you feel soft, just how I like a woman to be, and I'm glad you're not wearing a bra, it makes everything much simpler,' Dermid murmured, and she felt his nose nuzzling the hollow between her breasts which were on a level with his face. Then his lips were there, ravaging the deep cleft between the smooth rounded swellings of flesh and skin. 'You taste good, too,' he muttered thickly, and she felt his hand, which had slid under her shirt at her waist, clutch hold of her back painfully in an agony of pleasure, the finger-tips digging hard into her spine.

'No, Dermid, no!' she gasped, pushing and wriggling for all she was worth, only to find he had clasped her closely against him with both arms.

'Yes, Ellen, yes,' he whispered, his breath tickling her throat.

'But I don't want to, I don't want to,' she muttered breathlessly, even while her body was growing taut and hard, straining against the thrust of his, demanding to be possessed. Again she pushed with her hands and kicked out with her legs in an effort to regain her footing.

But it was useless. The more she struggled the tighter he held her, exerting the strength of his sinewy arms until she was sure he would crush her ribs and she could feel his laughter wafting across her face, rumbling deeply in his chest as they thrashed about, wrestling with each other until suddenly they were rolling off the low couch, still entangled with each other and falling to the floor. Then his mouth was against hers and he was pushing her back on to the fluffy sheepskin hearthrug, pinning her there with his weight, and the heat from the blazing fire was no hotter, no more consuming than the heat of his desire.

But desire was also leaping along her nerves, transmitted from the delicate probing of his fingers at her breast and from the sting of his teeth biting her lips. Groaning with pleasure, she groped inside the opening of his shirt, her fingers stroking and digging into the hard muscles of his shoulders which were sheathed in hair-crisped silken skin.

'That's better. Now we're getting somewhere,' Dermid murmured against her cheek, and she heard paper crackling between them as he moved sensuously against her.

'The will,' she muttered, and finding his ear close to her mouth she bit the lobe.

'To hell with the will,' he replied, and his hand groped down between them, hard knuckles brushing suggestively against her bare midriff and then against her skirt-covered stomach until he found the sheaf of papers and pulled it out. The paper rustled as he threw the will across the room. There was a muted thud when it hit something followed by a slithering sound as it slid to the floor. 'We have more important business to attend to,' added Dermid, his eyes opaque with passion, his lips parted and curving sensually, coming closer to hers as his hand slid up from her waist.

'Dermid, this is silly,' she protested firmly.

'You didn't used to think so, three years ago,' he whispered, rolling on to his side and pulling her with him so that they were lying face to face.

'But we were alone then,' she gasped, as her body seemed to turn to jelly at his touch, becoming completely beyond her control. 'We can't,' she whispered even as her hands sought the buckle on his belt and began to unfasten it. 'Not now, not here. Someone might come in.'

'I locked the door after you'd come in. Didn't you notice?' And again she felt laughter shaking him. 'Go on, Ellen, don't stop. Unfasten it,' he urged, and buried his face in the warmth of her throat.

'But we have to discuss the will. You said so and....'

'Later,' he groaned. 'Ellen, please....'

His lips were as hot as fire as they claimed hers again, and suddenly she was alight, burning with the flames of desire which had spread from him to her. Time and space became confused in her mind. She was back in her parents' log cabin, making love on the bearskin in front of the crackling birch logs on an afternoon in the fall, more than three years ago. And this was Dermid whom she loved with every quivering nerve of her body, every cell of her brain, Dermid, her dark-eyed, russet-haired chieftain, her torment and her love, without whom life was a wasteland, but with whom she had once reached the heights of ecstasy and with whom she could, would—no, *was* reaching again that wonderful, joy-releasing union of soul with soul, body with body....

With the heat of the fire at her back, the warmth of Dermid's body at her front as she lay with her head nestling against his shoulder, Ellen knew a sense of drowsy contentment and a reluctance to move. Paradise was this, here and now, lying close to him, feeling his fingers shift and tangle in her hair, lying there and not speaking because words were unnecessary now and could not improve upon perfection. Like this she and he were completely in harmony.

The phone bell jangled imperatively and Dermid sighed and muttered. Ellen raised her head from his shoulder.

'Forget it,' he commanded, and his fingers were hard against the side of her neck as he pulled her down.

'I can't,' she murmured as the phone rang again. 'Supposing it's your mother asking us to go and get Rowan? He can be a little devil when he wants and he might be driving her nuts.'

'Not my mother, he won't. Remember she's survived having to put up with me and then Angus.' Fingers under her chin, he raised her face to his and his lips were sweetly tender against hers. But still the phone rang irritatingly, disturbing their concentration, and after the ring came the loud rap of someone's knuckles on the door and the rattle of the knob being turned.

'Are ye in there, Mr Craig?' Bessie's voice boomed through the door panels.

At once Dermid rolled away and twisted to his feet, pushing his tousled hair back with one hand.

'You see what Bessie wants while I answer the phone,' he ordered, and began to buckle his belt as he went over to the desk.

Ellen got to her feet, fastened her blouse, pulled on her skirt and zipped it up. She stepped into her discarded shoes and walking across to the door she tried to smooth down her hair. She turned the key as quietly as she could in the lock and opened the door slowly only a little way, hearing Dermid speaking sharply and authoritatively into the receiver.

'Ach, were ye having a wee nap?' Bessie asked, her pale eyes flicking critically over Ellen's dishevelled hair.

'Well ... er ... sort of,' Ellen muttered self-consciously, and felt blood rush betrayingly into her cheeks. Heavens, she would have thought she'd developed enough poise by now not to give herself away by blushing! She was a twentieth-century woman who had been married for some years, not a Victorian miss. 'What do you want?' she asked, speaking more bluntly.

'Is Mr Craig there?' asked Bessie, trying to peer past her into the room.

'He's talking on the phone right now,' replied Ellen, refusing to open the door any wider. 'Why do you want to see him?'

'Ach, well now, James has come back with the car and Mr Craig said I was to let him know.'

'All right, I'll tell him.' Ellen began to close the door.

'But that isn't all,' persisted Bessie. 'That lass of Dr Menteith's is here wanting to see him.'

'Morag Menteith?' exclaimed Ellen, and instead of shutting the door in Bessie's face she stepped out into the hall and closed it behind her.

'Aye, the hard-faced brazen besom that she is,' said Bessie rather viciously. 'She scrounged a lift with James, so she did. Ach, I don't hold with young lasses hitch-hiking, and he ought to have had more sense than to take her up.'

'Why has she come here?'

'Now, how would I be knowing that? I've asked her and she won't tell me, just glares at me sullen-like and says she must see Mr Craig, says she phoned him earlier. She's in the kitchen—I told her to stay there. She was wanting to come with me, to walk right into the study, I've no doubt. But I soon put a stop to that. Ach, the manners of young folk today!' Bessie's eyes rolled expressively and contemptuously. 'But ye'd think she'd know better, wouldn't ye, having Dr Menteith for a mother?' She cocked a speculative glance at Ellen and came to some sort of conclusion. 'I'm thinking she's in some sort of trouble,' she added slowly.

'Then perhaps I'd better come and see her,' said Ellen.

'Now, that's a good idea,' Bessie nodded approvingly. 'Better for a young lass like that to talk to someone like you than to bother Mr Craig with her problems. And it won't do her any harm to find out there's a mistress in this house now and that she can't go barging in on Mr Craig just when she feels like it.'

'Has she come here before like this?' asked Ellen suspiciously.

'Yes, and it's high time she was put in her place, and you're the person to do it. She's been taking far too much for granted just because her mother is a friend of Miss Agnes.'

'And a friend of Mr Craig's,' put in Ellen dryly.

'Aye, that too,' agreed Bessie, her eyes narrowing shrewdly as she leaned forward and added in a hoarse whisper, 'Ye want to stick up for yeself now ye're here, Mrs Craig. Ye want to let 'em all see what ye're made of, and it'll soon put an end to all the guessing about you and Mr Craig. Shall I tell the lass to come and see ye in the lounge?'

'Er—yes, of course,' agreed Ellen weakly, and Bessie marched off back to the kitchen.

In the lounge Ellen sat on the window seat in the big bay window and stared out. The shrubs in the front garden were a-glitter with diamond drops as every tiny globule of rainwater caught on the thick evergreen leaves of holly and laurel reflected pale sunlight. Patches of blue in the sky were spreading wider and wider, pushing the purple-grey clouds apart, and beyond the garden the sand on the shore was changing colour, from drab greyish brown to dull gold, while the flat silken sea shimmered silver and turquoise.

'But I want to see Dermid, not her.' The voice was the same Ellen had heard earlier on the phone, soft and slightly breathless, its tone a little plaintive, and she looked round to see a small fair-haired young woman who was dressed in blue jeans and a navy blue duffle coat being pushed into the room by Bessie.

'This is Miss Menteith, Mrs Craig. Ye said ye would have a word with her since Mr Craig is busy,' said Bessie at her bossiest, all the time nodding and winking encouragement to Ellen behind Morag's back.

Taking her cue from the housekeeper, Ellen stood up and forcing a smile to her lips she went over to the girl.

'Do come in ... Morag, isn't it? I'm Ellen Craig. My husband is busy right now and I thought this would be a good opportunity for me to meet you. I've heard quite a lot about you.'

Behind the suddenly silent, open-mouthed girl Bessie gave one more approving nod before she left the room, closing the door firmly after her.

'You've heard about me? Who told you about me?

Did she?' Hands stuffed into the patch pockets of her duffle coat, Morag jerked her head back in the direction of the door through which Bessie had gone.

'No. My husband's aunt, Miss Craig, talked about you,' replied Ellen smoothly, grateful suddenly for the training Walter Stewart had given her in how to handle awkward people during an interview. 'She's very fond of your mother and she told me how you and Dr Menteith went cruising in the summer with Dermid. Did you enjoy the cruise?'

'Yes, it was a lot of fun, only....' The girl broke off and caught her lower lip nervously between her teeth. She was very pale, Ellen noticed, and her blue eyes were red-rimmed as if she had recently been weeping.

'Won't you take off your coat?' Ellen asked hospitably.

'No, I ... don't ... want....' Morag's eyes flickered anxiously about the room as if she felt trapped.

'Well, at least sit down for a few minutes, over here by the window. It looks as if the weather is clearing up, thank goodness. Did you have good weather when you were cruising?'

'Not bad. We were only caught once in a gale.'

'And there were only the three of you?' Ellen sat down on the window seat.

'Oh no, my younger brother Gavin was with us and ... and ... so was Angus.' Morag sat down abruptly on the other end of the window seat opposite to Ellen, her hands still in her pockets, chewing her lower lip, her eyes hidden by blonde lashes, spiky and stiff after being wet with tears.

'Angus Mackinnon?' asked Ellen.

'Yes.'

'I didn't realise Angus knew anything about sailing,' commented Ellen. 'I thought he only knew about farming and hunting.'

'He hasn't sailed much, but he's very strong and tough and that's why Dermid invited him to go on the cruise, to help with the putting up of the sails and pulling up the anchor,' said Morag. 'You see, Mother and I hadn't done anything like that before, so we weren't much help.'

'Perhaps you were invited to go along to help with the cooking ... a woman's job,' suggested Ellen dryly.

'Oh no, I don't think so. Dermid invited us to go ... because ... oh, I think he was being kind and trying to help Mother with my brother. You see, Gavin has been awfully difficult to handle since my father died last year. He's only fourteen and he misses Dad terribly and....' Again Morag broke off as her voice trembled.

'I understand,' said Ellen sympathetically, and Morag looked up slowly from under down-slanting eyebrows.

'You ... you're very different from what I expected you to be, younger and much prettier, much gentler,' she blurted.

'Oh, am I?' retorted Ellen with a laugh. 'Sounds to me as if Dermid has given you a bad impression of me!'

'Not Dermid,' said Morag, shaking her head. 'He never mentions you. In fact I didn't know he was married until Angus told me.'

'I see. Well, I can say also that you're different from what I expected you to be,' said Ellen thoughtfully. How wrong her image of Morag had been! No tall willowy blonde this, no white rosebud about to unfurl at the warm touch of love. The girl was awkward, her fair hair was limp and straggly and she was so thin Ellen suspected her of being undernourished. Hard to imagine Dermid with his appreciation of softness and grace in a woman being attracted in any way to this underdeveloped girl. Hard, too, to believe that Morag was the daughter of the tall graceful amplebosomed Ann. Ellen's hand clenched on the window seat as a vision of Ann's mature beauty flashed across her mind's eyes. Was it possible her guess had been wrong and it was the cool, collected blue-eyed doctor who attracted Dermid and not her daughter?

'Have you come back here to live with Dermid again?' The brazenness of the question touched Ellen on the raw and she stiffened.

'That's hardly any of your business,' she replied quietly.

'I should have guessed you'd say that,' said Morag with a sigh. 'Mum said the same when I asked her if she liked Dermid enough to marry him. Like her, you think I shouldn't be curious about the personal feelings of the older people I know. But I can't help it. I'm trying to find out why it is you all go about making one another unhappy. It makes me wonder when I hear about married people being separated or splitting up whether there's really something called love.' Morag's voice shook again and she looked down at the floor.

Ellen stared at the bowed fair head. The friendship between Dermid and Ann Menteith must be very well developed if Morag had been led to ask her mother such a leading question. As for the rest of what the girl had said, she sensed an appeal, a desperate appeal for reassurance, as if disillusion had already touched the vulnerable seventeen-year-old heart, and Ellen found herself remembering just how vulnerable it was possible to be at that age.

'Everyone said you'd come back to Dermid when you heard he'd inherited all his grandfather's money,' Morag muttered.

'Well, really! Everyone has had a good time talking about me,' Ellen said crossly.

'Isn't it true, then?' Morag looked up, her dark blue eyes glinting with interest.

'No, it isn't,' retorted Ellen fiercely. Here was her chance to stick up for herself and put an end to the guessing which had been going on about her and Dermid. 'And if you like you can tell *everyone* that Dermid asked me to come here,' she added slowly, thinking with a sense of surprise that it was true, because he had dictated that letter from Wallace Scott and he had said very recently in the study, *I wanted you to come*. He couldn't have said it more clearly and simply, and in the light of what had happened afterwards it was possible that he had meant it sincerely. 'And I came because I was tired of living apart from him,' she went on thoughtfully, explaining her own actions to herself as much as to Morag. 'I came because I want to live with him again and....'

She broke off and shot to her feet, her hands to her mouth, her eyes opening wide as she saw that the door had opened and Dermid was standing there staring at her and listening.

'Oh!' she gasped, and hurried over to him. 'Have you finished with the telephone?' she asked foolishly.

'Yes, I've finished with the telephone,' he replied, his mouth quirking with humour. 'It was the call I was expecting from the factory.' His narrowed gaze went past her.

At the sound of his voice Morag had bounded up from the window and was rushing towards him. Flinging herself at him, she burst out crying.

'Morag! What are you doing here? I told you on the phone that your mother wasn't here, that she would be back soon from her house calls and you should wait at home for her. She's going to give you hell when she finds out you've run away from school.' Hands on the girl's slight shoulders, Dermid pushed her away from him. Still sobbing, forlornly knuckling the tears from her eyes, Morag tried to speak, but couldn't.

'Do you know what's wrong with her?' Dermid asked, looking at Ellen.

'No. I ... I ... was trying to win her confidence so she would tell me when I saw you,' she explained, avoiding his intent burning glance.

'I liked what you were saying, Ellen,' he said softly.

'I'm not surprised,' she retorted defensively. 'It would fit in with what you expect your *wife* to say.'

'What riles me, though, is that you'd say it to her and not to me,' he countered, his mouth tightening as he turned to the sobbing Morag again. 'Come on, Morag, snap out of it,' he ordered curtly. 'What have you been up to now to bring disgrace on the name of Menteith and to add to your mother's worries?'

'I ... I ... oh, Dermid, you've got to help me, you've got to!' Morag flung herself at him again and this time his arms went round her comfortingly. 'I think ... I'm nearly sure ... I'm going to have a baby,' she sobbed.

Shock sliced through Ellen like a knife blade slicing through nerves and veins. She shouldn't be shocked, she found herself thinking objectively, because there was nothing new in a teenage girl confessing that she was pregnant. Then why was she shocked? Because the confession was being made to her husband, to Dermid, and he was being asked to help? He was looking very concerned as he pushed Morag away from him, gently this time, holding her by the shoulders and studying her tear-streaked face.

'When?' he demanded.

'I ... don't know. Next spring, I suppose,' muttered the girl.

'I don't mean when would the baby be born—if it is born, if you decide to keep it,' said Dermid in his cool practical way. 'I mean when did it happen?'

'When we were away on the cruise. You remember when we....' began Morag.

'Ellen, where are you going?' Dermid's voice cut across the girl's soft voice.

'To get Rowan, he must be wondering where I am.' Ellen kept her voice steady and cool as she opened the door.

'Can't you wait until I can come with you?' he asked. 'I can hardly leave Morag while she's in this state.'

'No, you can't, can you?' she retorted with synthetic sweetness. 'But don't worry, I can manage perfectly well on my own. I'm used to it.'

She shut the door, not with a bang but with a clear and final click to show she wasn't interested in being followed, and walked over to the stairs. Bessie was coming down and Ellen waited for the housekeeper to reach the hall before going up the stairs herself.

'Did ye have a word with the lassie?' Bessie's eyes held an expectant curious gleam.

'Yes. You were right. She is in trouble.'

'What sort of trouble?'

'The usual sort for a girl her age.'

'Ach, there's nothing new in this world.' Bessie shook her head.

'Bessie, I must go over to Auchinshaws for Rowan. Would James drive me there?' asked Ellen urgently before the housekeeper could ask any more questions.

'Aye, to be sure. That's why he's employed here, to drive people about, and it isn't as if he's overworked. When do you want to go?'

'In about five minutes.'

'He'll be waiting for ye at the side door.'

Ellen dashed up the stairs to the bedroom. Five minutes weren't really long enough for her to pack all three cases with the clothes she had brought for Rowan and herself, but it was all she could allow herself because she wanted to leave the house before Dermid appeared again and insisted on going with her to Auchinshaws. So she packed only the biggest of her cases with all she and Rowan would need for a couple of days. Later when she was settled at Sheila Moffatt's house in Ayr she would phone Bessie and ask her to send on the other cases and clothes to her.

She had to sit on the lid of the case to get it to close properly, it was so full. When it was zipped up and the straps were buckled she pulled on the wide-skirted narrow-shouldered calf-length camelhair coat she had brought with her and grabbing her handbag, which contained her passport and the return airline ticket, she staggered with the heavy case out of the room and down the stairs. The lounge door was still closed, so she assumed Dermid must still be comforting Morag. Her lips twisting wryly, she tiptoed past the door, down the passage to the side door.

James was waiting for her and didn't seem at all surprised when she handed him the suitcase. He put it in the boot and she climbed into the luxurious back seat of the Rolls. He took his place behind the steering wheel and the car purred quietly across the yard, through the gateway, and turned up the narrow lane to the main road.

Ellen leaned forward make sure James, who was slightly deaf, heard what she said.

'Is there a ferry leaving Portcullin for Wemyss Bay in the afternoon?' she asked.

'Aye, but ye've had that,' he replied. 'It left an hour ago, at two-thirty.'

'When is the next one?'

'Seven o'clock tomorrow morning. The ferry which arrives here at five o'clock today stays the night here and leaves then.'

'It there any other way I could get to Ayr?' she asked.

'Well, ye could be getting the bus to Glasgow and changing there,' he replied. 'But not today. There's only one bus a day and that leaves at ten in the morning. And then I suppose ye could be flying from Macrahanish.'

'Where's that?'

'It's a wee airport fifty miles from here.'

'Do you know anything about the flight schedule, the times of planes flying from there to Glasgow?'

'No, I don't. But ye could be asking Mr Craig. He knows.'

'But I won't be going back to Inchcullin House,' Ellen said coolly, and saw him glance curiously at the rear view mirror in which, presumably, he could see her face reflected.

'Won't ye now?' he muttered. 'Then where are ye going?'

'After we've collected Rowan from the farm I'd like you to drive me to Macrahanish airport.'

'Ach, I couldna' be doing that.'

'Why not? It isn't far and it won't take you long in this car.'

'It would take me a good two hours and a half

there and back and I'd have to be asking Mr Craig's permission to take ye. Ye see, he might be wanting the car himself to go somewhere this evening.'

'All right, then could you drive me to Portcullin after we've collected Rowan? Maybe I can hire a car there.'

'Aye, I suppose I could be doing that,' he replied grudgingly. 'Fergus Morrison at the hotel knows all about the times of the flights and he has a car to take people to the airport and from it.'

'Thank you.' Ellen leaned back and closed her eyes. Already she was feeling exhausted with the effort of trying to get away. How she wished she had ignored Dermid and had hired a car yesterday. If she had done that she wouldn't have to depend on James's half-hearted co-operation now. She would be on her way to Glasgow with Rowan never to return to Inchcullin, never to go back to Dermid.

CHAPTER SEVEN

AUCHINSHAWS was much as she had remembered it, walls shining white, windows seeming to blink lazily as they reflected the light of the westering sun which turned tawny harvested fields to gold and made dark blue shadows slant out from barns and pine trees. Sheep were bleating on the hillside and from a fenced field nearby came the loud bellows of an Ayrshire bull. As Ellen picked her way carefuly across the farmyard which had been churned into a mud-bath by the morning's rain, a sharp-nosed black and white sheepdog sprang out from a nearby outbuilding to dance around her, barking sharply and spattering her high-heeled shoes and nylon tights with mud.

'Down, Flash, down!' ordered a voice, and Ellen looked up to see Kate Mackinnon standing at the door of the house, tall and slim, dressed in a tartan skirt and a hand-knitted fair-isle jersey, her thick black hair looped back in a knot at her neck. 'Hello, Ellen,' she said, a faint smile curving her mouth, her dark glance going past Ellen to the parked Rolls. 'Has Dermid not come with you?'

'No. He ... he has a visitor, so I thought I'd better come on my own for Rowan. I hope he hasn't been too much trouble to you, Mrs Mackinnon.'

'A bairn is never any trouble to me, and he's a happy lad,' replied Kate. 'Ye'll stay for a cup of tea while ye're here,' she added, indicating that Ellen should step past her into the hallway of the farmhouse and closing the door. 'Come away, now, into the kitchen.'

'I ... er ... really shouldn't stay long,' Ellen said as she followed Kate down the hall. The first time she had met her mother-in-law she had wondered about Kate's age, she remembered, and she was wondering now. Kate was so much younger than her own mother, so young to be the mother of Dermid. She must have been only seventeen or eighteen when he had been born. Like Morag she had been caught young. Oh, God, she must stop thinking about Morag.

'Mummy, Mummy, look, look. I've got a puppy!' In the kitchen Rowan rushed up to her clutching a golden-haired Labrador puppy in his arms. It was all legs and big paws, struggling to escape from Rowan's awkward hold yet at the same time licking the boy's face with a long pink tongue. 'Uncle Angus gave it to me. He says I can keep it. I can, can't I, Mummy?'

Ellen looked down at her child's pleading face and felt a familiar feeling of helplessness rise up in her. How could she let him keep the puppy when she didn't know yet where they were going to spend the night? Silently she damned Angus for creating this new problem for her to solve.

'He's lovely, darling,' she agreed, crouching down in front of Rowan and stroking the puppy's smooth head, 'but I'm afraid you'll have to leave him here.'

'No, no! I want to take him home. I want him!' Rowan's chin wobbled and his eyes filled with tears. 'Uncle Angus says I can have him, didn't he, Grannie?' Rowan turned appealingly to Kate, who having filled the kettle was placing it over the burner she had lit on the gas cooker.

'Aye, he did.' She turned and looked at Ellen. How dark her eyes were, thought Ellen, how dusky her skin. No wonder Janet had called her a gypsy! 'Let him keep the puppy, Ellen,' Kate pleaded.

'But I can't.' Ellen stood up, and pushed her hands into the pocket of her wide loose coat. 'It isn't that I don't like it and don't want him to have it, but....' She broke off and drew a long deep breath. 'I can't let him take it because I'm going to stay with my mother's cousin in Ayr between now and Saturday when we fly back to Ottawa, and I know she doesn't like dogs,' she added in a hard flat voice, and stared defiantly at Kate.

The dark eyes didn't flicker once but gazed back at her steadily and just a little pityingly.

'I see.' Kate sighed and her glance went to Rowan's bright head. He was sitting on the floor hugging the puppy to him and talking to it. 'I'm sorry you're not staying at Inchcullin House longer. I'd have liked to have seen more of the bairn,' Kate went on quietly. 'Why do you have to go back to Canada so soon?'

She turned away to take cups and saucers down from the old-fashioned dresser.

'I have to go back to work,' said Ellen, still defiant.

'Your work is more important to you than Dermid is, then?' asked Kate as she set the cups and saucers out on the kitchen table.

'Mrs Mackinnon, please don't make any tea for me,' said Ellen urgently, ignoring the question because she didn't know how to answer it. 'I have to go now. James Blair is waiting to drive me into Portcullin. I'd like to get to Ayr tonight, if possible.'

Kate stood by the table, staring down thoughtfully at the tea-cups. Then she looked up and straight across at Ellen.

'You could leave the child here,' she said. 'I'll look after him. It's a pity to take him away so soon from the puppy.' She paused, then added with meaning, 'And from his father.'

'But I have to take him back to Canada with me,' blurted Ellen. 'He's mine....'

'And Dermid's,' said Kate softly, turning away to open the refrigerator.

'I have to go now,' muttered Ellen. 'I can't stay. Where is Rowan's parka, please?'

'Hanging in the porch.' Kate turned back to the table to put a jug of milk on it. Ellen opened the door to the back porch just as someone opened the other door. Angus stepped in bringing all the smells of the farmyard with him on his mud-caked rubber boots and his dark eyes glinted with surprise when he saw her.

'Hi,' she said to him, and went back into the kitchen to bend over Rowan who was still cuddling the puppy, 'Come along, darling,' she said firmly. 'Let's put the puppy in his basket.' She tried to lift the squirming bundle of golden fluff from Rowan's arms, but the boy hung on.

'No, no!' he shrieked shrilly. 'He's mine, he's mine. I wanna take him home!'

'But we're not going home right now,' said Ellen.

'Having trouble, Ellen?' Angus's voice was mocking. He had taken off his boots and his denim jacket and was rolling up his shirt sleeves as he made his way to the sink.

'Yes, I am, no thanks to you,' she retorted. 'He can' keep it, Angus. We're not going back to Inchcullin. Rowan, please let the puppy go. He's only a baby and he's getting tired of being pulled about you.'

'Going to Kilruddock, are ye?' Angus asked as he turned off the tap and began to wash his hands. 'Well the wee pup will be all right on the ferry. I've a travelling basket ye can put him in. He'll be easy to carry like that. I'll go and get it while ye're drinking y'r tea.'

Ellen stood up, temporarily defeated by Rowan's refusal to let go of the dog, and pushed her hair back from her forehead. It was warm in the kitchen and she was beginning to feel hot in her thick Canadian coat. Kate had made the tea and was covering the brown earthenware pot with a knitted cosy, and for a moment Ellen longed to give in, to sit down in the cluttered homely room to drink tea and forget her problems, pretend everything was all right between Dermid and herself. But it wasn't, it wasn't, and now it never would be.

'No, we're ... I mean Rowan and I aren't going to Kilruddock,' she explained. 'We're not staying ... oh, I might as well tell you both. I'm leaving Dermid for good. He can divorce me if he wants. I'm taking Rowan back to Canada and we're not coming back.'

Kate Mackinnon sat down suddenly on a kitchen chair, her sallow face suddenly very tired-looking, and Angus swung round to lean against the sink, his hands still wet and covered with soap-suds.

'Oh, Ellen, I can't help thinking you haven't tried very hard,' said Kate, sighing.

'What do you mean?' exclaimed Ellen, her hackles rising defensively as she sensed criticism.

'I mean that it seems to me neither you nor Dermid have tried hard enough to make your marriage work. You haven't lived together for three years, that's longer than you were together, and now after only a couple of days together you say you're separating for good. I can't help feeling you haven't given yourself or him much of a chance. You haven't been with him long enough,' said Kate quietly.

'I can't help that,' retorted Ellen. 'I have to go. I

can't live with him not after, not after....' She broke off and swung away so that neither Kate nor Angus could see the sudden trembling of her mouth and wishing she hadn't let herself be trapped into this conversation. She should have stayed outside, stood on the doorstep and let Kate bring Rowan to her there. She should have refused to enter the house.

'So the competition proved to be too much for you, eh?' Angus mocked. 'Ha, I'd never of thought you'd give up so easily.' And she whirled round to glare at him.

'It isn't a case of giving up,' she retorted. 'It's a case of facing up to reality.'

'Competition? What competition? Whatever are you talking about, Angus?' complained Kate in bewilderment.

'Ellen knows,' he drawled scoffingly as he dried his hands on a towel.

'Well, I don't,' said his mother crossly, and picking up the tea-pot began to pour tea into the big thick cups.

'Ach, come off it, Mother,' drawled Angus, pulling out a kitchen chair from the table, turning it around and then straddling it. 'You know all about Dermid and Dr Ann.'

'I've heard a lot of foolish gossip about them, that's true—ever since you and he took Dr Menteith and her children cruising in the summer. But I've heard some about you, too,' Kate gave Angus a sharp almost accusing glance, then looked back at Ellen. 'Surely you don't believe that Dermid and the doctor....' she began, then broke off to shake her head incredulously from side to side. 'Ach, as I say, it's just a lot of foolish gossip. Ann is too old, nearly as old as I am. She was only two classes below me at the primary school in Portcullin. She didn't get married and have children until after she qualified as a doctor, you see....'

'No, not the doctor,' said Ellen in a clear flat voice. 'The doctor's daughter.'

'Morag?' Angus's deep voice seemed to thunder through the room and he jumped to his feet. In two strides he was in front of Ellen, hands on his hips as he leaned threateningly towards her. 'Where the hell did you get that idea?' he rasped.

'Angus, please!' protested his mother. 'You don't have to be so rude!'

Just then there came a thumping sound on the ceiling and Kate also stood up.

'That's Grandfather Mackinnon, wanting his tea,' she announced picking up one of the cups of tea. 'Excuse me, Ellen. He's bedridden, you know. Don't go just yet. I'll be down in a few minutes....'

She went from the room and taking advantage of the fact that Rowan, disturbed no doubt by Angus's bullying tone, had let go of the puppy and had come to stand beside her, to clutch at her skirt and suck his thumb while he stared up at Angus with apprehensive eyes, Ellen began to push the child's arms into the sleeves of the parka.

'Come on, darling,' she said. 'We have to go now.'

'I want the puppy!' he wailed.

'I'll tell you what I'll do, Rowan,' said Angus, the tone of his voice altering quite amazingly. 'I'll keep the puppy here with me for a few days until he's properly house-trained. Ye wouldn't like it to be wetting all over the floor in your mummy's house now, would ye?'

Rowan shook his head slowly from side to side and as she zipped up the parka Ellen flashed Angus a grateful glance. He returned it with a mocking grin.

'*Now*, ye can tell me where ye've got the idea that there's something on between Dermid and Morag,' he whispered.

'From Morag herself, of course,' she retorted. 'Who else?'

'You've seen her?' he exclaimed, following her towards the door which led to the porch.

'Oh, yes, I've seen her, this afternoon at Inchcullin House. We had quite a talk,' said Ellen, pulling open the door and stepping out into the porch, 'until Dermid came into the room and then, of course, she lost interest in me, turned all her attention to him, was all over him in fact, in his arms, sobbing and crying, telling him she's going to have a baby.' Ellen wrenched open the back door, hearing Angus exclaim behind her, the same crisp expletive which Dermid used.

'Ye're sure?' he demanded urgently, holding the door back as she stepped outside. 'Ye're sure that's what she said?'

'Of course I'm sure. I'm not deaf,' she retorted tartly. 'No gossip this, Angus, but straight from the mouth of the competition. Do you wonder I'm leaving?'

'Because you believe Dermid is.... Ach, hell, no, Ellen!'

'Dermid is the father? Is that what you were going to say?' she challenged. 'Yes, I do believe it.'

'But why, in God's name why?' It seemed to her that Angus was very churned up about the whole business, and she couldn't understand why.

'Because usually the first person a woman tells when she knows she's going to have a baby is the father,' she said flatly. 'That's why.'

'But in this case you could be mistaken....' began Angus urgently.

'I don't think so. Goodbye, Angus. Say goodbye to your mother for me.'

Across the muddy yard she ran, pulling Rowan after her, knowing Angus couldn't come after her immediately because he was wearing only socks and would have to pull his boots on before venturing into the mud. Seeing her coming James Blair slid out of the car and opened one of the rear doors for her, and she thanked him breathlessly as she pushed Rowan ahead of her into the back seat.

The sky clouded over as the Rolls floated down the lane which led from the farm to the main road and raindrops spattered the windows. Yet the sunlight wasn't gone for ever. It kept coming back to gleam on the wet surface of the coast road to Portcullin and glitter on the wind-ruffled surface of the silvery sea. All the way to the fishing port sunlight and shadow alternated as they had throughout the last few days, ever since she had returned to Scotland, thought Ellen. And that was how the whole visit to Inchcullin had been, sometimes sunlit with joy, sometimes shadowed with unhappiness.

The car was just turning up a hill and about to dip over the other side into the town when the rainbow appeared, an arch of vivid colour in the blue-patched, cloud-rumpled sky, leaping over the hills, seeming to dip right into the sea.

'Oh, look, Rowan,' Ellen exclaimed. 'Isn't it lovely?'

'What is it?' he lisped.

'A rainbow. It comes only when the weather rains and shines at the same time. It's like a promise, a promise that everything will turn out right in the end.'

Her own words seem to mock her. Nothing was turning out right for her. Back in the study at Inchcullin, held closely against Dermid, she had begun to believe that it was possible, and that since they could love and laugh together again so they could live together again. And they had been loving and laughing on the rug before the fire. It had been a crazy, rollicking yet warmly tender coming together, quite unlike the violent, shocking union of the night before. It had been the sort that could only happen to two people who had once been very intimate and had become even more intimate with each other. It had held a wonderful promise for the future like the rainbow did, a promise which had broken up and had faded under the blast of Morag's announcement, just as the rainbow was breaking up now and fading fast.

'Did ye say ye would like to be set down at the hotel, Mrs Craig?' James Blair's voice interrupted her thoughts and she realised the car was passing slowly down the main street of the town, towards the harbour where lights in the fishermen's wharf were already blazing as the early November dusk crept across the sky.

'Yes, please,' she replied, and the Rolls slid to a stop in front of the entrance to the eighteenth-century coaching inn which was Portcullin's only hotel.

'Is Daddy here?' asked Rowan as he walked with her into the dimly lit foyer, and Ellen felt a jolt go through her. She hadn't realised that the few hours he had spent with Dermid would make such a deep impression on him that he would ask for his father. It was something new and hurtful she would have to learn to cope with until he forgot he had a father.

'No, he isn't,' she replied, and turned to James who had carried the heavy case into the foyer for her. 'Thank you very much, James. You don't need to wait around.'

He gave her a puzzled look from under his heavy grey eyebrows, but he didn't say anything, and Ellen was glad he had been trained not to pass comment on anything the people he drove about might do. No doubt later he would say something to Bessie, but right now he was blessedly non-committal.

'Just so,' he murmured. 'Then I'll be off back to the house.'

He raised his cap politely in farewell and went out. Ellen walked over to the reception desk. There was no one behind it and the whole place had a deserted atmosphere. On the counter top there was a small silver bell with a notice beside it suggesting she should ring if she wanted attention, so she picked it up and shook it.

'Mummy, I wanna go to the castle,' whined Rowan. 'I wanna see Daddy!'

Ellen stiffened and willed herself not to answer. She could see the next hour or two before she could put him to bed were going to be troublesome. She had to find the strength and patience to ignore his persistent demands, divert him in some way. She shook the bell again and heard with a sense of relief a door open and shut and then the sound of brisk footsteps on wooden flooring.

'Mummeee! Why can't I go to the castle? Wanna go in the car to the castle!'

Rowan took hold of her hand and tugged. She didn't move at all.

'Shush, darling, someone is coming,' she said.

There was a click of a light switch and lamps behind the counter and on it leapt on. A small woman in her early thirties had appeared and was stepping behind the counter.

'Now what can I be doing for you?' she asked cheerfully.

'I was wondering if Mr Morrison is here. I was told he could give me information about the flights from Macrahanish to Glasgow,' said Ellen.

'Ach, Fergus is away today and you won't be able to get to the airport in time for the next and last flight unless you have a car,' replied the woman. Her bright brown eyes were shrewd and curious as their glance flitted over Ellen and then flicked down to the thumb-sucking, bright-haired Rowan.

'But I thought—I was led to assume that the hotel provided transport to and from the airport.' said Ellen.

'Only in the summer.'

'Is there anywhere I could rent a car, then, to drive myself to Glasgow?'

'Not in Portcullin. I'm afraid ye'll have to be waiting here for the ferry in the morning or the bus.'

'I see.' Ellen could not help a sigh escaping from her and it took a lot of effort to keep her shoulders stiff and her head up. 'Do you have a room vacant where my little boy and I could stay for the night?'

'Well, we don't usually take visitors this time of the year. The season ended at the beginning of October.' Again the bright shrewd eyes went to Rowan. 'But if ye've nowhere else to stay I daresay I could make up the beds in the first floor front room.'

'What about a meal?'

'It would only be cold meats and pickles and I could be poaching an egg for the wee lad. Would that do?'

'Yes, thank you.'

The woman searched under the counter and brought out a wide flat book which she opened. She offered a pen to Ellen and said,

'Will you put your name and address in the register, please.'

Ellen scrawled her name and Rowan's and added her mother's address in Ottawa. The woman turned the book round and studied it.

'Are ye any relation to the Craigs of Inchcullin?' she asked.

'Yes.' Ellen braced herself for the inevitable questions, but the woman only gave her a strangely appraising glance before putting the book away and lifting down a key from the key board on the wall.

Half an hour later Ellen and Rowan sat at a table in the empty dining room and were waited on by the woman, who introduced herself as Mary Morrison, Fergus's wife. When she came to ask them if they had finished their meal she brought a girl of about twelve with her.

'Perhaps the wee lad would like to go with Fiona to watch the telly for a while,' she suggested. 'It's a children's programme and it'll give ye a wee break and maybe make him sleepy.'

To Ellen's relief Rowan went off with Fiona quite happily and she helped herself to more tea from the pot provided.

'He's very like his dad,' Mary remarked as she collected used plates together.

'You know Derm . . . my husband?' exclaimed Ellen.

'Aye. I went to school with him to the primary school here in Portcullin before his granddad sent him away to that boys' private school in Glasgow.'

Ellen set down her empty cup and rose to her feet, not wanting to become involved in any further conversation about Dermid.

'Is there a telephone I could use?' she asked. 'I

have to phone a cousin in Ayr to ask her to meet me off the ferry tomorrow. And could you tell me what time the ferry arrives at Wemyss Bay?'

'Weather being good it should be there at ten-forty-five, and the telephone kiosk is in the hall, near the stairs.'

It didn't take long for Ellen to find Sheila Moffatt's number and soon she was listening to the ringing tone. At last the receiver was lifted at the other end of the line and a man's voice spoke.

'Is Mrs Moffatt there?' she asked.

'No, I'm afraid she isn't. May I take a message for her?'

'This is Ellen Craig. Is that Ian?'

'Yes, it is. Ellen, where are you? Is this a transatlantic call?'

'No, I'm in Portcullin. I'm over on a visit and I was wondering if I could come and see your mother before I fly back to Ottawa on Saturday.'

'Och, I'm very sorry, Ellen, but that isn't possible. You see, my mother is away just now. She's gone on a cruise and won't be back until the end of March and tomorrow I'm off to Malaysia for a few weeks to supervise the installation of some new machinery in a textile mill, so I'm sorry I can't invite you to come over and stay. I suppose you've been staying at Inchcullin?'

'Yes. It's been nice talking with you, Ian. I'd better ring off now.'

'Mother will be sorry she missed you, but next time be sure to let us know when you're coming and then we can make arrangements to see you.'

'Yes, I will. Thank you. Goodbye.'

Ellen replaced the receiver and stood for a moment staring out of the kiosk. What should she do now? Where could she go for the next few days? The only other person she was on visiting terms with was Molly MacIntyre, her neighbour in Kilruddock, and she couldn't go there not now, not ever, because Dermid would be going there too. She would have to find a hotel she could stay in. Or maybe she could fly back before Saturday?

Quickly she opened her handbag and pulled out the airline ticket. On the folder she found the telephone number of the local office of the line and soon she was speaking to a clerk who had no trouble in changing the seat reservations for her and Rowan from Saturday's flight to a flight the next day leaving Prestwick at twelve-thirty. All she had to do was to find a taxi at Wemyss Bay to take her to the airport.

Her arrangements made, Ellen felt more relaxed and she went through to the small hotel lounge where Rowan was watching the children's programme with Fiona. She waited with him until the programme finished and was able to persuade him to go with her upstairs to have a bath, glad to find he had temporarily forgotten the castle and his daddy. Only when he was in the single bed tucked up with his eyelids dropping lazily over his eyes did he mention Dermid again.

'Is Daddy coming to sleep in that bed with you?' he asked.

'Not tonight.'

'Will we see him tomorrow?'

'Maybe,' she answered diplomatically, not wanting to disturb him with an outright no. 'Would you like me to read you a story?'

'Yes.'

She read one of his favourites and for a while his voice accompanied hers because he knew the words off by heart, he had heard the tale so often, but at last he stopped and glancing up she saw he was fast asleep.

She left the door open and the landing light on and went downstairs again to the lounge. Fiona had gone, but the television was still on, so she watched the end of the news programme. When it finished she wandered out into the hall. The drone of voices came from the direction of the bar which was now open for the evening. Looking for Mary Morrison, Ellen put her head round the door. As she had guessed, Mary was behind the bar pouring beer into a glass.

'Will it be all right if I go out for a walk?' Ellen asked her.

'Aye, just tell Fiona. She'll listen for the lad. She's in the kitchen doing her homework.'

Ellen collected her coat from upstairs and went to find Fiona, who agreed to listen for Rowan should he wake. She went back through the hall and stepped out into the street. A car was coming slowly down the hill and she heard it stop behind her as she walked towards the harbour.

The air was cool and damp, tangy with the smells of fish and salt-water. Ellen walked quickly and passed no one as she crossed over to the fishermen's wharf. The only sounds were the perpetual lap-lap of water against stone and the creak of the fishing boats as they pulled at their warps and shoved against each other.

In the dark opaque water the reflections of light winked and quivered, changing shape all the time, sometimes long and narrow, sometimes round like moons. In the distance at the end of the pier a mass of glittering lights was all that could be seen of the ferry.

Ellen walked as far as the wire fence which closed off the ferry terminal from the rest of the wharf. For a few moments she lingered, staring through the mesh. Tomorrow morning she and Rowan would leave on the ferry and this time tomorrow night they would be arriving in Canada, only it would be afternoon there because of the difference in time.

She shivered suddenly as the chill of regret swept over her and she seemed suddenly to ache in every bone. Tears welled in her eyes so that the ferry boat lights dazzled before her. She didn't want to go back. She didn't want to leave Dermid. Now that she had seen him again, had been with him, she wanted to stay and live with him no matter what he had done during the past three years and no matter what he might do in the future, because she loved him and would never love any other man but him. Then what was she doing here alone and miserable? Why hadn't she gone back to Inchcullin House?

Footsteps sounded on the stones of the wharf behind her. Quickly she brushed the tears from her eyes and pushing her hands in her pockets because they were beginning to feel cold she swung round to walk back to the hotel. Whoever was walking along the wharf had disappeared into the thick black shadows which were beyond the pools of greenish-white light shed by the high wharf lamps because she could still hear the crisp crunch of leather soles on stone even though she couldn't see anyone. Whoever it was couldn't be a fisherman, because a fisherman would wear rubber boots, surely, which would make a different sound. And now it seemed to her the footsteps were very close and the rhythm of them was familiar....

Her heart leapt suddenly in her breast as a tall figure stepped out of the shadow into the light shining over the fence and came towards her.

'Ellen, why didn't you came back to Inchcullin?' Dermid's voice was harsh. He came to a stop in front of her and she backed away from him, colliding with the wire-mesh fence. In the cruelly bright lamplight his face looked taut and angry, the lips thinned severely, the eyes glittering darkly. He had pulled up the collar of his suede jacket as a protection against the raw dampness of the air and had his hands in the slit pockets.

'How did you get here?' she exclaimed.

'James drove me here. We arrived just as you left the hotel so I followed you along the wharf. Why didn't you bring Rowan back to the house? Why are you staying at the hotel?'

'I ... I ... want to be near the ferry terminal so he and I can catch the seven o'clock ferry tomorrow morning.'

'You're going to Ayr to stay with Sheila? I thought I told you I don't want Rowan to go there and that he could stay with me while you visited her.'

'Yes, you did, but....'

'And this is your way of going against my wishes, I suppose,' he interrupted her roughly.

'No, it isn't. I'm not going to Ayr. Sheila isn't there—she's away.' Ellen drew a deep shaky breath and blurted, 'I've changed the reservations. Rowan and I are going back to Canada tomorrow instead of Saturday.'

Under the lamplight his face looked suddenly chalk-white and he flinched as if she had hit him.

'Like hell you are!' he grated. 'Why?'

'So ... so ... that you can get a divorce and marry that girl Morag Menteith.'

'So that I can *what*?' he demanded, speaking so loudly that his voice echoed back from the walls of the fish warehouse which overlooked the wharf. Taking a hand from a pocket, he took hold of her face, his fingers hard and warm against her chilled face, and turned it upwards to the light so he could study it. 'Are you out of your mind?' he asked, and in contrast to the way he had just yelled at her his voice was almost gentle.

'No, I don't think so.' She jerked her face free of his hold and his hand fell to his side. 'I've thought it all out,' she went on steadily, 'and I've decided I'm not going to be like my mother's cousin Barbara.' She saw his eyebrows meet over his nose in a frown of puzzlement. 'Your father's wife,' she explained. 'I'm not going to make it difficult for you and Morag as Barbara did for your father and your mother. As long as you agree to let me keep Rowan....'

'Ellen, I haven't the slightest idea what you're talking about,' he interrupted her again. 'But one thing I'm certain of, I don't want to marry Morag.'

'But you must,' she insisted. 'You can't let her child be born illegitimately. You can't!'

'Why can't I?'

'Well, because ... because it's yours and....'

'It is *not, damn you*! God, is that what you believe?' He drew a long hissing breath and his eyes glared murder at her. His hands shot out took hold of her shoulders and he shook her so hard that her head wagged back and forth like a rag doll's. 'You don't have a very high opinion of me, do you, Ellen,' he said between his teeth when he had finished shaking her, 'and all through listening to your mother and to Sheila Moffatt. Well, right now you're going to listen to me. I had nothing to do with Morag's pregnancy, do you hear? Nothing!'

Her head was still swimming as a result of the shaking he had just given her and the lights seemed to be swinging all about her, up and down, round and about, and she was glad he had hold of her and was still gripping her shoulders.

'Then why did she come to tell you about it?' she demanded.

'I don't know. I can only guess that she wanted to tell her mother and when she couldn't find her she came to me because she felt she could depend on me to take some sort of action.' His mouth curled bitterly. 'You see, some people do trust me, even if you don't.' He let go of her and pushed his hands into his pockets again. 'Also I think she was a little afraid of how Ann would react, and if you knew Ann better you'd understand why. She's very strait-laced and doesn't approve of permissiveness in any shape or form, and she's completely out of touch with her own children because she's always put her job as a doctor first. As a result her son is delinquent and Morag is ... well, you've seen her now and you know what's happened to her.' He slanted her a narrowed sardonic glance. 'And if you hadn't been so impatient, been in such a damned hurry to go to Auchinshaws you'd have found out more. You'd have found out that she believes Angus to be responsible for her present predicament.'

'Angus?' Ellen exclaimed. 'Then why didn't she go to him and tell him?'

'God knows,' Dermid shrugged indifferently. 'How do you expect me to know how the female mind works?' he added with a touch of self-mockery. 'Perhaps she was afraid he would laugh at her and deny they'd ever been together. But they had plenty of opportunity for it when we were on the cruise. They were always going off somewhere together.'

'Where is Morag now?'

'With her mother.'

'Angus knows about her,' she muttered. 'I told him.'

'You did?' His eyebrows lifted in surprise. 'Why?'

'Because ... oh, because he asked me why I believed

something was going on between you and Morag,' she whispered.

'And just how did you get around to discussing that?' he drawled threateningly.

'I ... I ... told your mother and him that I couldn't stay and live with you any more and he made fun of me—you know what a tormenting devil he can be.'

'What did he say?'

'He accused me of giving up because the competition was too much for me. He ... he ... meant Ann Menteith and I ... I ... told him it was Morag and not Ann ... oh, Dermid, please don't look like that! I'm sorry. I'm sorry I jumped to the wrong conclusion, truly I am.'

'Sorry!' he exclaimed bitterly. 'You think saying sorry can cancel out what you've believed about me? I ought to walk away from you here and now, go and get Rowan, take him away from you before you can turn him against me....'

'No, you wouldn't be so cruel,' she cried, her hand on his arm to stop him as he swung away from her.

'Wouldn't I?' he countered, swinging back to glare at her with angrily glittering eyes. 'Just try pushing me any further, Ellen, and you'll find out how cruel I can be, as cruel as you are and have been ....' He broke off and stared at her narrowly again. 'You know, you've behaved very strangely ever since we met at Prestwick. You've been on the defensive all the time as if there's something you don't want me to know about you. And then there's been this lack of trust almost as if you've been hoping to find a reason for ending our marriage which you can blame on me. You want me to be the guilty party in any divorce proceedings. And yet this afternoon I was quite sure we were getting close to resolving our particular problem, and when I heard what you were saying to Morag in the lounge....'

'I was only saying that to put her in her place,' she blurted, her pride stepping in again. 'She'd said everyone has been saying I've only come back because you've inherited your grandfather's money and Inchcullin, and I was trying to make it clear to her that nothing was further from the truth by telling her I'd come back only because you'd asked me to come.'

'So you didn't mean what else you said, about coming back because you were tired of living apart from me?' he challenged.

'That came out without thinking,' she evaded.

'Because it was what you were feeling, perhaps?' he suggested softly, putting his hands on her shoulders gently this time and beginning to draw her towards him, bending his head.

'Oh, it isn't fair, it isn't fair!' she protested, her hands on his chest to hold him off.

'What isn't?' he asked, ignoring her resistance and touching the corner of her mouth tantalisingly with his.

'Every time we should be discussing what we should do you move in on me to kiss me ... and then ... and then I can't think straight any more. No, Derm....' He cut off the name with his mouth, covering hers, and she felt a quicksilver sweetness run through her. Before she realised it her hand was at the back of his neck and their mouths held together hungrily as if they had only just met. When he lifted his head it was like coming out of a warm enchanted place into the cold damp air of the night to the feel of the soft Scottish rain on her face.

'Doesn't that tell you something about us, Ellen?' he murmured in her ear. 'Doesn't it tell you that we still want each other even after nearly three years of separation, that the flame of desire is still leaping between us, brighter and stronger than ever?'

Her heart was thudding noisily in her ears. He was doing it again, she warned herself, trying to overwhelm her with that power he possessed. Why? Why? She had to find out why, and to do so had to move away from him. She stepped back, her hand dropping to her side. With a twitch of her shoulders she freed them from his light grasp and stepping sideways, her back still to the fence, she inched away from him.

'Desire, yes, but not love,' she said. 'If you'd ever loved me you'd never have suggested a separation.'

'And the answer to that is this,' he retorted coldly. 'If you'd loved me, really loved me, you'd never have let the separation go on so long. It was up to you to end it, to say when you'd had enough of being free and independent.' He paused, turned up the collar of his jacket again and thrust his hands into the pockets. 'Ellen, if there's someone else ... over there you're in love with why don't you come out with it, say so?' he said slowly. 'Then we'll take it from there.'

She turned to him, lifting her face so that the harsh light shone down on it, glinting on the raindrops which spangled her skin—and perhaps on the tears?

'There isn't anyone,' she whispered. 'There's never been anyone else.'

'Then it's the job. It's more important to you than being married to me. Is that it? Is that why you want to go back tomorrow?'

The blunt forthright questions were bewildering her. Didn't he realise he had only to say a few short words and her pride would collapse?

'I ... er ... I'm not sure,' she muttered. 'Oh, I don't know, and I'm getting wet standing here. I'm going back to the hotel.'

She set off, walking quickly, her head bent to the rain, her shoulders hunched. Not once did she look round to see if Dermid was following her. There was no Rolls-Royce parked at the kerb outside the hotel and as she pushed open the door to go into the foyer she wondered vaguely where James had parked it. The hallway was as dim as ever, only one lamp being on behind the reception counter, and as Ellen stepped forward she blundered into something on the floor, banging her shins, losing her balance and falling forward, hands outstretched and landing on what was obviously luggage. Feeling bruised and breathless, she moaned miserably. It seemed that nothing was going right for her.

'What happened?' Dermid's voice was surprisingly near and concerned. His hands were on her arms and he was helping her to her feet, drawing her against him to hold her closely. 'Are you all right?'

'I wasn't looking where I was going and I tripped over somebody's luggage,' she muttered, leaning against him.

'Our luggage, yours and mine,' he whispered. 'I told James to leave it here, but I thought he'd have more sense than to leave it in the way. Are you sure you're all right?'

'Yes. I bruised my shins, that's all, and probably laddered my stockings.' She pushed away from him so that she could see his face, lean-boned and shadowed, with a bold nose and a wide humorous mouth which was now set in a taut line of control, and the eyes dark and different, alien and mysterious, hinting that he wasn't always cool and practical, not always in control of his feelings. 'Why did you bring my other cases?' she asked.

'I thought you might be needing them wherever

you're going. And I brought mine because wherever you're going I'm going with you.'

'Even if I go to Canada?' she challenged.

'Even if you insist on going there.'

'But what about your work? You said you had only two days off.'

'I know I did, but when my boss phoned me today I told him not to expect me back this week, that I'd decided to spend more time with my wife and son.'

It was suddenly too much for her and she covered her face with her hands.

'Oh, I don't understand you any more,' she whispered. 'You've changed so much.'

'No, not really, Ellen. I've learned to love you while we've been apart, that's all.'

She raised her face from her hands and stared up at him incredulously. His mouth twitched in self-mockery.

'Sounds crazy, doesn't it?' he drawled, and she nodded, still staring at him. He glanced round the hall. 'Is there somewhere where we can sit, alone, where it's warm?'

'The lounge?' she suggested rather diffidently, almost afraid to move in case the magic spell in which she seemed to be caught broke; in case she had been mistaken and Dermid hadn't said he loved her after all.

The fire in the lounge fireplace was burning well and there was no one in the room. Ellen took off her wet coat and draped it over a chair, then went to sit on the settee in front of the fire and hold out her cold damp hands to the warmth. After taking off his suede sheepskin-lined coat Dermid came over to the fire too, but he didn't sit down. Leaning an elbow on the white-painted wooden mantelpiece, he stared down at the flames.

'You were right just now, out there on the wharf when you said that I didn't love you when I suggested a separation. I didn't. Not properly, not enough to share you with a job or even with a child, not enough to stay married to you,' he said quietly.

'Then why had you married me?' she demanded hoarsely, feeling fresh pain stab through her.

'You know why.' He moved suddenly to squat before her, supporting himself with both hands on the cushions on either side of her thighs. On a level with hers, his eyes glowed redly like the half-burned coals in the fire. 'I wanted you. I wanted you so badly, and it was the one sure way I could get you. If I hadn't proposed marriage when I did you'd have gone back to Canada at the end of your holiday before I could....' He broke off and his hands slid along her thighs, fingers tightening, clenching on her skirt-covered, rounded limbs. 'I just wanted to possess you and I didn't give a damn for the future, I didn't care that you were not ready for marriage. I didn't care what it would do to you. I thought only of myself.'

'I don't want to hear any more,' she muttered, shaking her head from side to side. 'I don't want to know.'

'But you must know. I have to tell you before I can even hope you'll be willing to start all over again.'

'You mean ... you want me to come back to you?' she whispered.

'I mean I'd like us to live together again,' he said steadily.

'For Rowan's sake?'

'Partly, but mostly because I'd like to be your lover and your husband again, because I'd like you to be there fretting and fussing about how long I'll be gone when I go away. I'd like you to be there when I come back and I'd like to have the right to fuss and fret when you go away, to be there when you come back. You see, Ellen, I've discovered while we've been separated that unless you're part of my life it isn't worth living.'

'Then why didn't you ask me to come back before?' she exclaimed, and he gave her a strangely wary under-browed glance.

'I have to admit that when we were first separated I was glad to be free for a while,' he said. 'It was great to be able to come and go as I pleased again without having to consider anyone else, and it was with some reluctance that I wrote to you at the end of that first year.' He gave a short slightly bitter laugh. 'But your reply came as a shock. It seemed I wasn't the only one who was enjoying being free. You were too.'

'And that was when you decided to hell with me, I suppose,' she suggested coolly, leaning back away from him. Although in one way she welcomed his honesty it was still hurting to realise how little she had mattered to him at first.

'That's right.' His mouth curled cynically. 'I thought I could easily find someone to take your place, but that didn't work, and as time went by and you didn't show any signs of wanting to end our separation it became harder and harder for me to sink my pride and ask you to come back. I could only ask you to bring Rowan and hope that when we met again we'd both find out how we really felt about being married to each other. Then Grandfather died and his will gave me a chance to contact you again.'

'I still think you tricked me into coming,' she accused.

'I have no regrets,' he retorted. 'You came.' He levered himself up on to the settee beside her, not touching her but sitting sideways with his head resting against the back close to hers as he watched her. 'I used to think about you in the night,' he said softly. 'I used to lie awake and try to remember the way your mouth is, the way your nose tilts, the way your lashes curl, the way you laugh and the way you cry. I thought my memory was pretty good, but I didn't remember your mouth right. Are you going to give me the chance to learn it all over again, Ellen?'

Slowly she turned her head to look at him so that their faces were almost touching.

'We've been such fools, both of us, silly stubborn proud fools,' she whispered, raising her hand to trace the curve of his upper lip. 'I used to lie awake and think of you too and remember how it was with us, the lovely times we had together, the pleasure we'd known with each other. I love you, I've loved you all the time, but I pretended I didn't because I guessed you didn't love me. Oh, when I think of all the days and nights we've wasted, being apart!'

'They weren't wasted,' he said, sliding a hand up her arm to her shoulder slowly and suggestively, over her shoulder to her neck where his fingers moved against the sensitive skin below her ear, delicately tantalising her. 'Think of that time apart as being necessary to us both. You had to find out if you could do that job, and you have. I had to find out what loving you was all about, and I have.'

Their lips met tentatively at first, then more demandingly as passion leapt up in both of them. For a while the only sounds which saved the room from being silent were the fall and hiss of coals in the grate and the distant beat of recorded music coming from the hotel bar.

'Ellen, Ellen, go easy,' whispered Dermid at last,

wrenching his mouth from hers, 'or you know what will happen.'

'Yes, I know, but it's such a relief to show you I love you. I wasn't sure before, you see, about you.'

'You're sure now?'

'As sure as I'll ever be.'

'Then perhaps you'll tell me how many beds there are in that room you've booked here.'

'Two, one double and one single.'

'And will I have to shift Rowan out of the double into the single?'

'No. He's in the single already. He wanted to know if you were going to share the other bed with me.'

'He doesn't miss much of what's going on, does he?' he said with a laugh. 'What did you tell him?'

'No, of course, because I'd no idea you'd follow me here.'

'I've told you I'm going wherever you go, even to Ottawa if I can get a seat on that plane tomorrow.'

'But I'm not going there,' she said, tantalising in her own way.

'Then where are you going?' he demanded, frowning at her.

'To Kilruddock, to our house, to start all over again,' she replied, rubbing her nose against his cheek.

'What about your job?'

'Walter said I wasn't to go back if I didn't make a clean break with you. He said you were on my mind, and he was right, but I don't want to make a clean break with you, not now.'

'And not ever, because I'm not going to let you.' Dermid's fingers tightened bitingly on the back of her neck.

'Oh, how domineering and possessive you've become!' she complained teasingly.

'And how bossy and argumentative you've become,' he retorted tauntingly.

'I can see we're going to have lots of fights.'

'What if we do? It won't matter as long as we're together again, as long as we love each other enough to forgive and never to forget....'

'You've got it wrong,' Ellen argued. 'It's forgive and forget.'

'Why don't you wait until I finish what I have to say before arguing?' he taunted, his mouth close to hers again. 'As long as we forgive and never forget the pleasure and the happiness we've known together, we'll stay together. Don't you agree, sweetheart? Isn't that what it's all about?'

'Yes,' she agreed wholeheartedly, 'that's what it's all about.'

Titles available this month in the Mills & Boon ROMANCE Series

RETURN TO DEVIL'S VIEW by *Rosemary Carter*
Jana could only succeed in her search for some vital information by working as secretary to the enigmatic Clint Dubois — and it was clear that Clint suspected her motives ...

THE MAN ON THE PEAK by *Katrina Britt*
The last thing Suzanne had wanted or expected when she went to Hong Kong for a holiday was to run into her ex-husband Raoul ...

TOGETHER AGAIN by *Flora Kidd*
Ellen and Dermid Craig had separated, but now circumstances had brought Ellen back to confront Dermid again. Was this her chance to rebuild her marriage, or was it too late?

A ROSE FROM LUCIFER by *Anne Hampson*
Colette had always loved the imposing Greek Luke Marlis, but only now was he showing that he was interested in her. Interested — but not, it seemed, enough to want to marry her ...

THE JUDAS TRAP by *Anne Mather*
When Sara Fortune fell in love with Michael Tregower, and he with her, all could have ended happily. Had it not been for the secret that Sara dared not tell him ...

THE TEMPESTUOUS FLAME by *Carole Mortimer*
Caroline had no intention of marrying Greg Fortnum, whom she didn't even know apart from his dubious reputation — so she escaped to Cumbria where she met the mysterious André ...

WITH THIS RING by *Mary Wibberley*
Siana had no memory of who she really was. But what were Matthew Craven's motives when he appeared and announced that he was going to help her find herself again?

SOLITAIRE by *Sara Craven*
The sooner Marty got away from Luc Dumarais the better, for Luc was right out of her league, and to let him become important to her would mean nothing but disaster ...

SWEET COMPULSION by *Victoria Woolf*
Marcy Campion was convinced that she was right not to let Randal Saxton develop her plot of land — if only she could be equally convinced about her true feelings for Randal!

SHADOW OF THE PAST by *Robyn Donald*
Morag would have enjoyed going back to Wharuaroa, where she had been happy as a teenager, if it hadn't meant coming into constant contact with Thorpe Cunningham.

Mills & Boon Romances
– all that's pleasurable in Romantic Reading!

Available September 1979

DON'T MISS SEPTEMBER'S
GREAT DOCTOR - NURSE ROMANCES

SISTER IN OPPOSITION *by Linda Shand*
Sister Alison Palmer did not take slights without attacking right back — whether it was standing up to her unfriendly superior or getting her own back on the arrogant Richard Langford with a kiss which set the hospital grapevine aquiver! But she didn't count on Richard's swift and cunning revenge...

DEAR DOCTOR EVERETT *by Jean S. MacLeod*
Janet's youthful friendship with Martin Everett was just a far-off memory; certainly it seemed no reason why it should prevent her from marrying Ellis, the brilliant surgeon, to whom she owed so much — until Martin suddenly came back into her life.

LOOK OUT FOR THEM AT YOUR NEAREST
MILLS & BOON STOCKIST

Forthcoming Classic Romances

A GIRL ALONE
by Lilian Peake

Sparks had flown between Lorraine Ferrers and Alan Darby from the moment they met — and it was all Lorraine's fault, for not trying to conceal her prejudice against him. Then, unwillingly, she found herself falling in love with him — but hadn't she left it a little late?

JAKE HOWARD'S WIFE
by Anne Mather

Jake Howard was immensely attractive, immensely rich, immensely successful. His wife Helen was beautiful, intelligent, well bred. A perfect couple, in fact, and a perfect marriage, everyone said. But everyone was wrong . . .

A QUESTION OF MARRIAGE
by Rachel Lindsay

Beth was brokenhearted when Danny Harding let her down, and vowed that it would be a long time before she fell in love again. But fall in love again she did — with Danny's cousin Dean, a very different type of man indeed, and one who really loved her. Or did he? Surely fate wouldn't be so cruel as to strike Beth again in the same way?

WHISPERING PALMS
by Rosalind Brett

The discovery of mineral deposits on her African farm came just at the right time for Lesley, but besides prosperity, it brought a scheming sister determined to get most of the spoils herself and to marry the most eligible bachelor in Central Africa.

Mills & Boon Classic Romances

— all that's best in Romantic Reading

Available October 1979

Forthcoming Mills & Boon Romances

CHATEAU IN THE PALMS *by Anne Hampson*
Philippe de Chameral could have made Jane happy — but he did not know that she was a married woman ...

SAVAGE POSSESSION *by Margaret Pargeter*
Melissa had been too used to having her own way to allow Ryan Trevelyan to dominate her — but she soon had to change her tune!

ONE MORE RIVER TO CROSS *by Essie Summers*
Rebecca was as different from her flighty cousin Becky as chalk from cheese, but the girls' identical appearance was to get Rebecca into a difficult situation with the bossy Darroch ...

LURE OF EAGLES *by Anne Mather*
An unknown cousin had inherited the family business, and Domine found herself agreeing to the masterful Luis Aguilar's suggestion that she accompany him to South America to meet the girl.

MIDNIGHT SUN'S MAGIC *by Betty Neels*
Could Annis ever make Jake see that she had married him for love, and not on the rebound?

LOVE IS A FRENZY *by Charlotte Lamb*
Seventeen-year-old Nicky Hammond's devotion was touching, but Rachel couldn't possibly return it. Yet how could she convince his disapproving father Mark that she wasn't cradle-snatching — or worse?

THIS SIDE OF PARADISE *by Kay Thorpe*
Gina's so-called friend was after a man with money, so Gina couldn't really blame Ryan Barras when he got entirely the wrong idea about her ...

A LAND CALLED DESERET *by Janet Dailey*
LaRaine had always been able to twist men round her finger but, as luck would have it, she fell in love with Travis McCrea — who had no time for her at all!

TANGLED SHADOWS *by Flora Kidd*
Kathryn could hardly refuse to return to her husband when she learned from his family that he had lost his memory in an accident — but would he remember what had destroyed the marriage in the first place?

THE PASSIONATE WINTER *by Carole Mortimer*
Piers Sinclair was her boy-friend's father: older, more sophisticated, far more experienced than she was. And so of course Leigh fell in love with him ...

— all that's pleasurable in Romantic Reading!
Available October 1979

Cut-out and post this page to order any of the
popular titles (overleaf) from the exciting NEW

Mills & Boon
Golden Treasury
COLLECTION

EXCLUSIVE, DIRECT-DELIVERY OFFER

BRAND NEW — Exclusive to regular Mills and Boon readers only on DIRECT-DELIVERY ORDERS by post! This unique series brings you the pick of our all-time, best-selling romances by top-favourite authors... all newly republished, in a thrilling new format, as the MILLS AND BOON GOLDEN TREASURY COLLECTION.

See overleaf for details of 10 wonderful titles — all available NOW at just 50p each! HURRY! Make your selection NOW and place your DIRECT-DELIVERY ORDER below.

Post to: **MILLS & BOON READER SERVICE, P.O. Box No. 236, Thornton Road, Croydon, Surrey CR9 3RU, England**

Please send me the titles I have ticked ☐ overleaf from the NEW Mills and Boon Golden Treasury Collection.

I enclose £.......... (No C.O.D.) Please ADD 18p if only ONE book is ordered. If TWO (or more) are ordered please ADD just 10p *per book*. MAXIMUM CHARGE 60p if SIX (or more) books are ordered.

Please write in BLOCK LETTERS below

NAME (Mrs/Miss) ....

ADDRESS..

CITY/TOWN...

POSTAL/ZIP CODE......................................

* Readers in Australia and New Zealand please note that these titles are available only through membership of Romance Book Club, PO Box 958, North Sydney, NSW 2060

*South African and Rhodesian readers please write for local prices to P.O. Box 11190, Johannesburg 2000, S. Africa.

ORDER NOW FOR DIRECT DELIVERY

Choose from this selection of

Mills & Boon
Golden Treasury
COLLECTION

- ☐ GT51
  COME BLOSSOM-TIME, MY LOVE
  Essie Summers

- ☐ GT52
  WHISPER OF DOUBT
  Andrea Blake

- ☐ GT53
  THE CRUISE TO CURACAO
  Belinda Dell

- ☐ GT54
  THE SOPHISTICATED URCHIN
  Rosalie Henaghan

- ☐ GT55
  LUCY LAMB
  Sara Seale

- ☐ GT56
  THE MASTER OF TAWHAI
  Essie Summers

- ☐ GT57
  ERRANT BRIDE
  Elizabeth Ashton

- ☐ GT58
  THE DOCTOR'S DAUGHTERS
  Anne Weale

- ☐ GT59
  ENCHANTED AUTUMN
  Mary Whistler

- ☐ GT60
  THE EMERALD CUCKOO
  Gwen Westwood

ONLY 50p EACH

SIMPLY TICK ☑ YOUR SELECTION(S) ABOVE, THEN JUST COMPLETE AND POST THE ORDER FORM OVERLEAF ▶